A Pony for
Jean

A Pony for Jean

JOANNA CANNAN

Illustrated by ANNE BULLEN

HOT KEY BOOKS

Published in Great Britain in 2014 by Hot Key Books
Northburgh House, 10 Northburgh Street, London EC1V 0AT

A Pony for Jean first published by The Bodley Head in 1936

A CIP catalogue record for this book is available from the British Library.

ISBN: 978-1-4714-0450-4

Typeset in 12.5pt Caslon by Palimpsest Book Production Limited,
Falkirk, Stirlingshire

Printed and bound by Clays Ltd, St Ives Plc

www.hotkeybooks.com

Hot Key Books is part of the Bonnier Publishing Group
www.bonnierpublishing.com

FOR ALL CHILDREN WHO RIDE;
ALL CHILDREN WHO WOULD RIDE
IF THEY COULD; BUT ESPECIALLY
FOR THOSE THREE INTREPID
THOUGH UNORTHODOX HORSEWOMEN,
JOSEPHINE, DIANA AND CHRISTINE.

I

WHEN I heard that we were going to leave London and live in the country, I was miserable. I can't believe that now, and I am sure that, if you are country children, you can't believe it either, unless you have already made up your minds (which I hope you haven't) that I was an awful little Rosemary-Ann sort of girl with curls, and frills, and frocks down to my feet at parties. I wasn't a bit like that really, though I must confess that I was always rather clean and tidy, but that was Nurse's fault, because she was always brushing and combing me, and Daddy's fault too, for being rich – as he was then – and being able to afford new clothes for me, and a nurse who had nothing to do but brush and comb me. I can tell you it is an awful nuisance having rich parents.

It may seem impossible to you, but really I had never been in the country. In the holidays Daddy and Mummy used to go abroad, and I used to go with Nurse to seaside places where there were promenades and sand and other London children – places like Westgate and Frinton. Of course I liked them because there was bathing and sand, and I was awfully young then and didn't know that there are places with rocks and boats and fishermen; and in the same way I didn't know that there are nicer places than London. Of course, we did the nicest things there. In the summer we used to have picnics in Kensington Gardens, and I used to sail my boat on the Round Pond, and in the winter we used to go and feed the ducks in the Serpentine, and sometimes we went down to the river and fed the seagulls. It sounds fearfully feeble now that I know what it's like to have your own animals, but I didn't know anything in those days and really it wasn't my fault if nobody told me.

When Mummy said at breakfast that we were going to live in the country, I couldn't eat any more, and as soon as I could I went out into the garden. I loved the garden though I can see now how awful it was: in the country, tiny two-roomed cottages have bigger gardens. The part nearest to the house had been paved and made fashionable so it wasn't any good to play in, but at the other end there were two big plane trees, and, though nothing would grow under them, people had had to leave them there because they hid the sordid backs of a very ugly row of houses. Between the fashionable part of the garden and the plane trees, there were some laurel bushes. They were always covered with soot and they smelled of cats when you crawled among them, but they were thick and secret: even Nurse couldn't see through them from the windows.

Behind the laurels and under the plane trees I had my hut, that a sentimental aunt had given me on my sixth birthday. It was called a 'Wendy House,' and you were supposed to play Peter Pan in it. Of course I didn't play

Peter Pan. Sometimes it was a shack in the Wild West, and sometimes it was a log hut surrounded by my enemies, and sometimes it was a crofter's hut in the Highlands where I harboured Prince Charlie. It was never a Wendy House except when Aunt Daphne came to tea with Mummy.

I went straight to my hut on that fatal morning. Shadow, our black cocker Spaniel, came with me. It was all rather complicated because Mummy had said that we had to go to live in the country because Daddy had lost his money in pepper; and an awful thought came to me that perhaps we wouldn't be able to afford a licence for Shadow or his dinners. The hut was in a frightful mess because the day before it had been surrounded. There were corpses of honest seamen all over the floor – of course they were only Teddy Bears and dolls really.

Shadow and I hadn't the heart to tidy up. We sat down and mourned among the corpses. It made me feel funny inside to think of going away and leaving the plane trees and the secret laurels. Whoever bought the house would be sure to cut down the laurels because laurels are Victorian; I don't know why, but that's a fatal thing to be. It seemed so awfully ungrateful to go away and leave the laurels to their fate when they had always been so obliging and hidden me from Nurse with their poor, ugly, sooty, Victorian leaves.

I cried about the things in the garden and then I began to think of the things outside. I thought of the ducks in Kensington Gardens. There were three I liked best and I had named them Lucy, Emily and Henry after the children in the Fairchild Family. I thought they would miss me when they didn't see me coming any more with bits of bread for them in my little green basket. Of course I didn't know then that they were probably terribly overfed and had enlarged livers, and would get on much better without me and my little green basket.

Well, presently Mummy came out into the garden. She was looking worried, which I don't like, and she stood in the fashionable part and called, 'Jean!' I called back, 'What?' which Nurse always said was rude, and Mummy came round the laurels. I dried my eyes hastily on Shadow's ears, which are useful for that; and Mummy came into the hut and said, 'Don't you know that Mademoiselle is in the schoolroom?'

Mademoiselle was the French person who used to teach me so that I should have a good French accent. That's another tiresome thing about having rich parents – you have what grown-ups call 'advantages.' They think that you are very lucky and ought to be grateful, but I have tried both and I can tell you that it is much more fun to go to an ordinary school and have a bad French accent like other children.

I said, 'Can I take Shadow in with me?' and Mummy said, 'You'd better not. Mademoiselle doesn't like him. She says dogs smell.'

I hugged Shadow and buried my nose in his fur because I liked his smell. I didn't know then that it was the smell that all gun dogs have – a country smell. I expect you

4

know it. It is heaven to meet it again when you come home for the holidays or if you have had the misfortune to stay a few days with your Aunt in London.

SHADOW

Mummy stood still for a minute, apparently forgetting that Mademoiselle was in the schoolroom. Then she said, 'Well, anyhow, Shadow will like the country. There'll be rabbits, Shadow, and . . . and rats.' Mummy had always lived in London. She didn't know any more about the country than I did then.

I said, 'Oh, shall we be able to keep him?' and Mummy said, 'My good girl, we shan't be as poor as all that. Of course we shall be able to keep Shadow and we shall have to have hens.' She said (as though it's the only thing you have to do about hens), 'You will be able to go round with a little basket and collect the eggs.'

I saw myself going round with a little basket. There were buttercups and daisies in the picture. I didn't know then what hens were.

Mummy spoilt the picture by remembering Mademoiselle in the schoolroom. She said, 'Well, beetle off, darling,' so I beetled off, thinking of hens and feeling much more cheerful. I went across the fashionable part of the garden, up the iron steps and through the greenhouse into the schoolroom. I saw at once that Mademoiselle was in a bad temper. Mummy told me afterwards that it was because she had just heard that we couldn't have her any more because of pepper.

I am not going to tell you anything about lessons because nobody wants to hear them even mentioned. I don't suppose that you want to read about London either, so the next chapter will begin when we got to Hedgers Green.

II

I WISH I could tell you all the exciting things that happened to us when we first went to the country, but if I did, this book would be too long for anyone to read and too expensive for anyone to buy except people who are still rich, and Mummy says that they are few and far between. It would take volumes to tell you all about the ducks and the geese and how we bought a wife for Shadow, and how, when I still didn't know about shutting gates, a herd of bullocks walked into the garden and ate all our greens at six o'clock in the morning.

In the weeks before we left London, Nurse was always saying how dull it would be for us in the country and Mademoiselle said it would be 'très triste' and that we should die of 'ennui.' But we hadn't been at Hedgers Green for a week before we found out that we were living in a whirl of excitement. The hen house roof, which was corrugated iron, blew off and sailed over the lawn and smashed the dining-room window; Sally, Shadow's future wife, came, and she ate my sponge and it swelled up inside her; I fell into the duck pond and came out green, and a runaway horse, with twelve tiny pigs in its cart, came past our gate and Mummy stopped it. In fact, we soon found out that every day in the country something happens, and it's not like going to the Cinema or to museums and seeing what happened to other people: the things happen to you – they're your own adventures. So, as I can't tell you about everything that happened to me at Hedgers Green, I am going to tell you about the most interesting thing of all, and that was – riding.

I must explain first that we looked for a house near Hedgers Green because we had cousins who lived there, and those were the days when we thought the country was dull and Mummy said that it would be nice to know *someone*. I knew the cousins a little because when they were in London buying clothes for school or going to the dentist, they used to come and have lunch with us, and they were all right as long as they were eating, but after lunch it used to be awful: they hardly ever spoke except to Shadow, and when they had finished speaking to him they used to stand at the window looking out and grumbling because there were no horses in London. There were two boys, Guy and Martin, and a girl called Camilla, who was a year younger than I was. Camilla didn't grumble about the horses, but she used to wriggle and say why should she wear tight clothes to come up to silly old London? Sometimes the cousins had toothache and that made them worse than ever. Nurse hated them, but she said what could you expect when they lived in the country and never went anywhere or saw anything?

I should have been sorry for my poor country cousins if they hadn't seemed to despise me. They looked scornfully at my toys and said that my hut would hold twenty-four bantams or a dozen hens. Camilla never wore socks except in the depths of winter, and she asked me why I did, and I said because I was made to. Camilla said that once they had bought her a pair of socks and she had thrown them up on the stable roof and they had stuck on the weather-cock. The gardener had got them down and then she had put them on the horns of the Ayrshire bull and nobody had dared to get them off again. Of course I had no stories like that to tell to Camilla.

I don't think the cousins were at all pleased about our coming to live near them. Mummy and I went to tea with them as soon as we had finished moving in and getting our small white cottage tidy. The children were all at home; it was almost the last day of the summer holidays. Their house was big, though it wasn't a baronial hall or an ancestral castle; and they had a huge garden and lots of fields and a lovely wood where they had huts that they had made them-selves. They were allowed to light fires there and cook things. But they weren't making fires that day. They were riding.

Cousin Agnes met us at the gate and she said, 'Come along. The children are in the paddock.' We went across the lawn to some white railings. On the other side of them was the paddock. Jumps had been put up there, hurdles with gorse stuck into them, and an imitation stile, and poles that you could make higher and higher. The cousins were jumping their ponies. They didn't stop when they saw us, but waved scornfully.

Cousin Agnes began to tell me about the ponies. She said that Guy's black one was a five-year-old that his father had given him on his last birthday. Its name was Blackbird. Martin's pony was called Red Knight. It was a roan cob, quite old but very clever. Camilla was riding a lovely little chestnut with a white star on its forehead. It was called after the evening star – Hesperus.

Hesperus was being very naughty. He wouldn't jump the stile and he bucked when Camilla tried to make him. Mummy said, 'Isn't he rather lively?' and Cousin Agnes said, 'Oh, Camilla's all right. She can ride anything.' I was looking at the ponies, the black and the roan and the chestnut flying along with the wind in their manes, and suddenly I wanted, more than I wanted puppies even, to hear someone say, 'Oh, Jean's all right. She can ride anything.'

Cousin Agnes said, 'I expect you'd like to help unsaddle the ponies, Jean,' and she shouted to the cousins, 'Come along in now. It's tea time.' Then she and Mummy went indoors and I stayed by the railings.

The boys went on jumping, but Camilla rode over to me. She said, 'What was Mummy saying?'

I said, 'She said you were to come in now. It's tea time.'

Camilla said, 'Bother. It's always something.' She turned round and yelled at the boys, 'Tea time!' Then she said to me, 'Do you like Hesperus? Would you like to try him?'

I said, 'I don't know.' I expect you will think that I was very silly and babyish, but you must remember that I had just seen Hesperus bucking.

'SHE CAN RIDE ANYTHING'

'Well, do you or don't you?' said Camilla in despising tones.

Camilla is a year younger than I am and I felt furious, and Camilla's despising me seemed worse than anything Hesperus could possibly do. I said, 'Yes, I should like to try him,' and I started to get on.

Camilla said, 'That's the wrong side. And when you get on you should face the tail.'

I said, 'Don't teach your grandmother to suck eggs.' This was very silly, because Camilla knew all about riding and I didn't and it would have been much more dignified to have said so. I blush now when I think of it.

Camilla said, 'Oh, all right, I won't then,' and let go of the bridle, which she had been holding. I scrambled on and gathered the reins up anyhow.

Guy cantered up to me.

'I say, can you ride?' he shouted.

Of course I couldn't. I had only ridden ponies at the seaside where a boy ran beside you. But though Hesperus felt very bouncey under me and not at all like the seaside ponies, I was still so furious with Camilla that I shouted back, 'Yes, of course.'

Guy stopped his pony and sat there looking at me and grinning and suddenly I felt as if something had burst inside me. I was all rage right down to my toes and the tips of my fingers. I did the maddest thing. I pulled Hesperus round and rode towards one of the jumps at a canter.

I think Guy shouted at me, but I didn't take any notice. I rode towards the jump and it looked very high and suddenly Hesperus's mane and his little chestnut ears rose up in front of me, and the next thing I saw was the ground coming to meet me. There was an awful thump and I knew no more till I woke up on the sofa in the drawing-room.

I woke up rather slowly. The first thing I heard was Cousin Agnes scolding Guy. 'You're a perfect fool,' she said. 'You ought to have stopped her,' and she said to Mummy, 'Claire, I shall never forgive myself. I can't think why I've got such idiotic children.'

I said, 'It wasn't his fault. He asked if I could ride and I said yes. It was my fault – really.'

Everyone turned round then and looked at me. I saw to my surprise that Camilla was crying.

Cousin Agnes said nothing, but she handed me a glass of water. I drank it and then I began to think what a fool I must look lying on the sofa like an old lady. Then I thought it didn't matter much what I looked like. For ever and for ever the cousins would despise me.

Mummy said, 'Well, it certainly was your fault if you said that, when you've only ridden seaside ponies. But perhaps it was worth it.' She quoted from poetry, *One crowded hour of glorious life is worth an age without a name.* I didn't know what it meant then, but afterwards at school it was explained to me, and I agreed with it, and I always write it when people with autograph books ask me to write in them.

Cousin Agnes said, 'Well, I daresay it's the right spirit, but it's made my knees knock and I could do with a cup of tea.' Once when I was in Kensington Gardens with Nurse, and Shadow had a dogfight with a Sealyham, my own knees had knocked, but it had never occurred to me that such a thing could happen to a grown-up. Somehow I think it was then that I began to like Cousin Agnes.

Mummy said, 'I should think that my idiot-child had better stop in here on the sofa.'

I knew that I had acted like an idiot, so I couldn't be offended, but I couldn't stay on the sofa any longer and be treated as if I was ill. I jumped up and said, 'I'm all right.'

The room was whirling round me, but it stopped after a bit and no one knew.

We all went into the dining-room and I was only allowed a slice of thin bread and butter and a cup of tea. But there was a plate of cucumber sandwiches near me and I managed to get four.

Mummy and Cousin Agnes talked at tea and nobody else said anything. But when we had nearly finished, Guy said suddenly, 'If she wants to ride she might have The Toastrack.'

Cousin Agnes said, 'Oh, Guy, how can you?'

Camilla said, 'The Toastrack's mine.'

Guy said, 'He's not yours any more than he's mine or Martin's. You were only saying yesterday that you wouldn't be seen dead on him.'

Cousin Agnes said, 'Well, it's an idea. At least if Jean wants ever to ride again. Do you, Jean?'

I didn't know whether I did or not. My neck was beginning to ache and in my imagination I could still see the ground coming to meet me. But I remembered what had happened the last time I said, 'I don't know,' so I said, 'Yes,' with firmness.

'The Toastrack's awful,' said Martin. He had red hair and freckles and always said what came into his head without stopping to think whether it was polite or suitable. 'Daddy bought him out of kindness. He's been half starved and he's all over horse bites. He simply won't go. He can't jump either. We've tried him and he just crawls over leg by leg.'

'He sounds just the pony for Jean then,' said Mummy. 'But I'm afraid that just now . . .'

That is a polite way of saying that you have no money. But Cousin Agnes said hastily, 'My dear, if Jean would like him she can have him as a gift. Honestly he isn't worth anything. Your orchard would do him proud and you only need bring him in in the depths of winter. Nigel could easily spare you a load of straw occasionally and some hay. He would be all right for Jean to start on, but I'm afraid he's exactly as Martin describes him.'

'It's awfully good of you, Agnes,' said Mummy. 'What do you think, Jean?'

I thought that even if The Toastrack was awful and all over horse bites, he would be better than nothing; anyhow he would have a velvet nose and the smell of horses. What had happened was that in spite of being so stupid and pretending I could ride, and falling off and fainting and lying like an old lady on the drawing-room sofa, I had begun that afternoon to love horses, and once you've started you can't stop, and you would sooner look at the ugliest horse than at the loveliest pantomine, and you would sooner hear the sound of hoofs than the most beautiful music, and you would sooner smell the smell of stables than the scent your mother used to have when she was rich, that came from Paris and was called Enchanted Evening and cost a guinea for quite a tiny bottle.

I was eating one of my sneaked cucumber sandwiches. I swallowed it nearly whole and said, 'Oh, please let's have him.'

Cousin Agnes said, 'Oh, well, that will be very nice then, but I warn you he's no picture. Guy can bring him down to-morrow. Unless,' she said, for she was one of the few people who understand how awful it is to wait for anything exciting, 'you would like to take him home with you?'

'Oh yes, please,' I begged her.

She laughed and said, 'All right. If everybody's finished, we'll go and look at him.'

There was a terrific scraping of chairs and we all got up and went out into the garden and down the drive to the stables. Cousin Agnes said, 'He's out all night, but we bring him in in the middle of the day because the flies worry his sore places.' And as we got nearer to the stables, she added, 'Now prepare yourselves for a scarecrow.'

I went into the stable first. It was cool and dark after the sunny garden and it smelled lovely. I thought it was empty at first and then I saw that in one of the loose boxes there was a bay pony eating busily. He was frightfully thin. His hip bones stood out and he had two grooves running down his hindquarters, which I was told afterwards are called 'poverty marks.' He was a bay pony but his coat was all rusty and dusty and he looked a dull ugly brown, and his tail, which was black, was straggly and bald in places. I stood at the door looking at him and he turned his head round and looked at me. Now that I know his dear face so well and have groomed every hair on his body, it is difficult to remember him as he was then, but I shall never forget the long soft look he gave me.

The others came in, and Guy opened the door of the loose box. Most of us went into the loose box and the thick straw rustled. Guy said, 'I'll give you a leg up,' and I scrambled on The Toastrack's back. His backbone stuck out in a sharp ridge and was very uncomfortable to sit on.

Cousin Agnes told Mummy that he was over thirteen hands, and somewhere between seven and nine years old. She said, 'Really I feel ashamed of giving you such a dud. Jean must start on him and then we must see what we can do about a better pony.'

I suddenly felt that I didn't want a better pony. I was a dud too. I felt for The Toastrack.

Guy was awfully decent. He said, 'We've got an extra brush that you can have and a curry comb. Do you know how to groom a pony?'

I said, 'No,' humbly.

Guy went to get the brush and the curry comb, and Mummy and Cousin Agnes faded away to look at the garden. I don't know how they could, when they might have been looking at the dear Toastrack.

When Guy came back he was simply loaded. He had a saddle and a bridle and a halter as well as the brush and the curry comb. He put the saddle and bridle down and gave me the brush. He told me to lean all my weight on it when I was brushing, and he said that you got awfully hot and should dismiss any groom that you saw grooming a horse with his coat on.

'I SHALL NEVER FORGET THE LONG SOFT LOOK HE GAVE ME'

Presently Mummy and Cousin Agnes came back and Mummy said that we must be going. Guy put on the saddle and Camilla put on the bridle and Mummy took the halter and the brush and comb.

This time I mounted on the right side and facing the tail.

The Toastrack walked very slowly down the drive and stood stock still at the gate while we were saying goodbye and thank you. When I tried to get him out into the road he wouldn't move, so Mummy led him. She said it was a funeral procession but I didn't mind. I could hardly believe that I was riding home on my own pony.

I said, 'I'm jolly well not going to call him The Toastrack. How would Camilla like to be called Snubnose or Martin Freckle-Face?'

Mummy said that it was certainly enough to give him an inferiority complex. In case you don't know, that means thinking you are stupider or uglier than other people, and it must be very uncomfortable. So as we went slowly along we tried to think of a beautiful name for him.

I thought of Sir Lancelot and Buccaneer and Bonny Dundee, but Mummy said that The Toastrack might get just as bad an inferiority complex from feeling that he couldn't live up to his name. She suggested countryfied names: Lad's Love and Sweet William and Harvester. Then we got silly and giggled and suggested names like Haystack and Midden and Mangle-Wurtzel and Corrugated Iron. You know how silly you can get if you start giggling. I rolled about in the saddle and nearly fell off and Mummy's legs went weak and she leaned against The Toastrack and he stood still.

We decided not to be silly and we went firmly on. I still giggled at intervals. Then, as we were going through the village, we met some horrible boys. They pointed at The Toastrack and said that we were taking him to the knacker's and he would be made into sausages.

I was awfully angry with them. I didn't take any notice, but looked at The Toastrack's ears. He didn't take any notice either, but just walked slowly on. He reminded me of someone going to the scaffold and ignoring the rabble, and when he had passed the boys I said to Mummy, 'I know. Let's call him Cavalier.'

Mummy thought that that would do, so we decided. I have heard since that it is unlucky to change a horse's name, but I don't believe it, because I have never had any bad luck with my darling Cavalier. And his name must have been altered twice at least, because the cruel master, that he had before the cousins bought him out of kindness, didn't call him The Toastrack, but probably something dull like Jack or Tom.

When we got back to our cottage the sun was setting, and under the apple trees in the orchard it was shady and cool. We turned Cavalier out there and at once he started eating. We stood looking at him for ages and then I had to go in to supper and bed. But I could see him out of the bathroom window as I dried myself, eating happily under the round harvest moon.

III

I WOKE up at six – at least, Bluey, my clock, said that it was six, but since I dropped him over the bannisters he is apt to be half an hour or even a whole hour slow. Usually I am bad at getting up, but that morning I leaped out of bed and it didn't take me a minute to put on my Aertex shirt and my shorts and my sandshoes. I crept downstairs and let myself out of the back door into the garden. It was a fine morning, and everything was covered with dew.

I ran to the orchard gate and there was Cavalier still eating. I called him and he threw up his head and looked at me. I ran back indoors and got five lumps of sugar and the bridle, which I had hung up in the hall.

Then I went back to the orchard and through the dewy grass to my pony. I gave him three lumps of sugar and stroked his poor thin neck. Then I began to put the bridle on.

Putting a bridle on is as easy as winking the third or fourth time you do it, but it is perfectly awful the first time, especially if you have no one with you to show you how. I took the snaffle in both hands and Cavalier opened his mouth most obligingly, but every time I got the bit in,

'I RAN TO THE ORCHARD GATE'

the bridle slipped down. When I let go of the bit to take hold of the bridle, the bit fell out of Cavalier's mouth and I had to unmuddle the bridle and start again. I got hot and bothered and Cavalier began to jerk his head about. If you get hot and bothered your horse always does too.

When I had tried six times and was really despairing, I heard a laugh on the other side of the hedge that separates the road from the orchard. For one awful moment I thought it was the cousins who had got up early and come down to see how I was getting on. But when I looked I saw it wasn't the cousins but the old man who looks after the hedges and ditches on the road. I had already made friends with him and he had told me that he had been a carter for forty years.

When he saw me looking at him he said, 'Lor' bless you, Miss, that baint the way to bridle an 'orse.'

I said, 'Oh, Mr Perks, I wish you'd show me,' and he opened the orchard gate and walked in.

He showed me how to put my hand under the snaffle and hold the head-band in the other hand. I had Cavalier bridled in two seconds.

Mr Perks stood and looked at Cavalier and said that he was poor, he was, but he'd pick up, no doubt, and he said that he'd been a good 'un and that a drop of blood was worth two ton of bone. Then he said he must be off or them there grass edges would be growing right over the road, and he gave me a leg up and went away looking like part of the country and the early morning, and not like a person at all.

'I GOT HOT AND BOTHERED'

I can't tell you everything that I did every day with my pony, because, as I said before, this book mustn't be too long, and if I told you everything I should have to leave out some of the really exciting things that happened later. A few days after I had brought Cavalier home, I started going to Miss Pringle for lessons. Miss Pringle lived in the village. She was a retired schoolmistress. She was quite

CAVALIER LOOKING OUT

old and generally much better tempered than Mademoiselle. She lived in a red brick villa like a dolls' house and kept a canary called Stanley after Mr Baldwin, and a cat called Mary after the Queen.

Every morning before I went to Miss Pringle I used to go into the orchard and fetch Cavalier into the stable. It wasn't a smart stable like the cousins'. It was built of flints and mortar and it leaned sideways, but everyone in the village, whom we consulted, said that it would last these forty years. Inside there were two stalls divided by a very old crumbly wooden partition, and in each stall the floor, which was brick, was worn away in four places by the hoofs of the carthorses, who had stood there for the last three hundred years. Daddy knocked down the partition between the stalls to make a loose box, and we hoped that we should find old coins between the boards, but of course we didn't. However, we had a very nice big loose box, and we sawed the door across so that the top half could stay open, and when I came back from Miss Pringle the first thing I used to see was Cavalier looking out, and really he looked quite like a first-class hunter with his bones hidden by the lower half of the door.

Uncle Nigel sent us some hay and straw, and he sent some oats and bran and a hay-bag too. Cavalier used to have the hay when he was in the stable during the day. Mr Higgins, the farmer, told me that flaked maize was fattening, so I bought some with the ten shillings Daddy had given me on my birthday, and we mixed it with the oats and the bran. Then we read in a book, which Mummy bought second-hand for sixpence, that boiled barley was 'useful for getting a bit of flesh on a poor horse,' so Cavalier had that too. Out of the same book we learned how to make a bran mash and Cavalier had one every Sunday for his tea. Of course if your pony is nice and fat there is no need to give him any of these things. He will do quite nicely on grass and hay.

'AT FIRST I STAYED IN THE ORCHARD'

It was only in the mornings that I used to go to Miss Pringle. Every afternoon I rode Cavalier. At first I stayed in the orchard and Mummy used to come out with the book, which had pictures of good riders and bad ones, and she used to tell me which I was looking like. I took three days to learn to rise in my stirrups and I thought that I should never learn, and then quite suddenly it came. The next day I went beyond the orchard. I didn't go into the road because

I wasn't sure if the cousins had gone back to school yet, and I thought that I might meet them riding beautifully on their fat and frisky ponies. I went into the fields at the back of our house, where there is a footpath which leads nearly three miles to Mr Higgins's farm. Half-way along this footpath there is a stile, which will come into my story again presently, so please remember it; but the field gates were always open, so, if you were riding, you could go in at one gate and out at the next and avoid the stile.

I learned to canter along the footpath. At first it was difficult to get Cavalier to canter because he was so thin and tired, but every day he seemed inclined to go a little further and a little faster, and one morning at the end of the first fortnight we were encouraged by the voice of Mr Perks saying over the hedge, 'Lor' bless me, I do see a change in that 'orse, to be sure.' Both Mummy and I had thought that Cavalier was fatter, but when you look so often and anxiously it is difficult to tell. Daddy only came down for the week-ends at that time because he was busy in London seeing if any of the family fortune could be saved, so we had hoped that he would be able to tell us, but he wouldn't take any interest in Cavalier. Mummy told me in secret that it was because he hated not being able to buy me a better pony, which was silly, because I wouldn't have swopped Cavalier for the most beautiful and expensive pony in the world.

After about a month I felt quite at home when I was cantering and not in the least tempted to hold on to the saddle or to Cavalier's mane, which, by the way, was getting

'I HAD THOUGHT CAVALIER WAS FATTER'

much thicker. I wondered what a gallop would be like, but I thought it would be cruel to make Cavalier gallop until he was feeling much more lively. Then I thought of jumping, but Mummy said no; she had had enough of that when I fell off Hesperus. She said I must wait till Daddy could afford to pay for proper lessons. I argued and argued and then Mummy said that I should drive her into a lunatic asylum, so I had to give in. I don't know why grown-ups are always so nervous. I am sure that when I have children of my own, I shan't be.

I suppose it was very wrong but one day, when Mummy was out, I did try jumping. I made two pillars of bricks that were lying about in the orchard and I put a bean-pole across them. Cavalier was very obliging and he trotted briskly up to the jump, but he only went over it leg by leg as the cousins said he would do. I got off and found some more bricks and made the jump higher, and he trotted up to it again and just knocked the bean-pole away with his forelegs. I tried him again and again, but he did the same thing every time, and unfortunately I forgot to take the jump down when I went in to tea. Mummy found it and there was what Nurse used to call 'unpleasantness,' and I was told that Cavalier would be sent back to the cousins if I tried to jump him again.

The unpleasantness blew over, as it always does in the end, though sometimes when it is happening you feel that nothing will ever be the same again, but about a week later there was some more unpleasantness, because, when Miss Pringle was out of the room and I was supposed to be doing fractions, I drew horses in my arithmetic book, and when Mummy came to fetch me, Miss Pringle complained. Considering it was the first thing I had done to annoy her, I thought that she was very mean, and when Mummy said how tiresome I was, I answered, 'What's the use of arithmetic, anyway?'

Mummy said that I ought to learn everything I could, because when I was grown up I would have to earn my own living because of pepper, and I said that I was going to be a horse-breaker and break horses by kindness instead of by frightening them, and you didn't have to know arithmetic to earn your living that way. Mummy said how could I be so silly as to talk about breaking horses when I had only ridden for two months on an old screw.

I was *furious*. Lately I had felt that the time when someone would say, 'Oh, Jean can ride anything,' was getting nearer, but now it seemed very far away.

When we got home from that unpleasant walk, I went into the orchard and talked to Cavalier. He was out all day now because there are no flies in November, and we hadn't yet begun to bring him in at night because of the cold. I am sure he knew that I was miserable, and that it wasn't only because he expected sugar that he nuzzled me so. The afternoon passed miserably. It poured with rain and Mummy wouldn't let me ride. I sat and read a silly book about some children who were always forgiving each other and kissing, and, while I was reading, Sally, who was still a puppy then, ate my hat, and Mummy was annoyed. She said how could a person sit in a room with a dog eating a hat and not notice it? and I said, 'Quite easily,' and she said she would tell Daddy that I was getting very rude. She told me afterwards that she was worried that day because pepper had gone worse than ever. Grown-ups are funny. I wish that, instead of making a fuss about hats and arithmetic, she had told me what was really the matter, at the time.

We had tea in gloomy silence and then I shut up the hens. Our ideas about collecting eggs in little baskets had vanished, and there was plenty of room in my coat pocket for the solitary egg I found. Before I went back indoors, I went to say goodnight to Cavalier. I had hung his hay-bag on a tree because I thought the ground was rather wet for him to eat off, and there he was tearing the hay out and not eating it at all, but wastefully throwing it down. I would have given him a lecture on wastefulness only I had heard enough lectures myself that day. I put my arms round his neck and he agreed with me that hats didn't matter and that one day I should be able to ride anything, and I told him I should always love him best no matter how many beautiful and valuable horses I broke in.

Then I went back to the house and finished the book about the sloppy children. Then I stood about till it was bedtime. The bath water was cold, as it always is at the end of an unsuccessful day.

I went to bed and I dreamed that Miss Pringle was a horse and she sat at the table and turned the pages of a book with her hoofs and neighed. In the middle of the dream I heard Mummy say, 'Ssh. Wake up but don't speak. There's a burglar downstairs.'

I woke up thinking that Mummy was part of my dream, and then suddenly I knew that the part about Miss Pringle was a dream but the part about Mummy was true. She was leaning over my bed, quite like the ministering mother in the book about the sloppy children. She hadn't brought a candle, but I could see her quite plainly, for the moonlight was streaming into the room.

I whispered, 'Ooh.' In my imagination I could see the burglar downstairs, creeping silently from room to room.

'Shall we go down and capture him?' I suggested.

'No,' said Mummy. 'That's no use. He's much stronger than we are. I locked the door when I came in, and anyhow, I don't for a moment suppose that he'll come up here. Only it does seem silly to let him get away with it. I wonder what we could do? We can't telephone because he's downstairs.'

'Can't we shriek "Thieves! Fire! Murder!" out of the window?' I suggested.

'There's no one to hear,' said Mummy, 'except the hens.' She giggled and then she had an inspiration. 'I know,' she said, 'we'll get out of your window and slide down the roof and run to the farm.'

'Yes!' I said, and I got out of bed.

'You must put on some clothes,' said Mummy.

'Why?' I said. 'You haven't got anything on.'

This wasn't what Daddy would call an 'accurate statement'

for she had on a pair of black satin pyjamas, that had come from Paris in the days of our richness. But of course you do not mince your words when there is a burglar downstairs.

I had blue pyjamas on. They were flannel and much thicker than Mummy's satin ones. But she seized my sweater, which was on the floor, and pulled it over my head and handed me my shorts and my shoes and stockings, and I tugged them on.

My room was at the back of the house. It had an attic window and below the window the thatched roof went down nearly to the ground.

Mummy took my eiderdown off my bed and wrapped it round her. Then she squeezed through the window. She stuck rather, and I could hear her saying words that I am not allowed. While she was sliding down the roof, I looked out. The moon was very bright and I could see Cavalier eating under the trees. Suddenly I had an inspiration. I tip-toed to the door and got down the bridle, which, since the first day, has always hung in my room.

Then I squeezed through the window quite easily and slid down. It was lovely. I forgot all about the burglar. The thatch was cold and smooth to slide on and it was splendid to be sliding down a roof under the moon.

Mummy was ready to catch me but I dropped quite gently on the grass.

I held up the bridle and whispered, 'Look! It'll be much faster if I go on Cavalier.'

'But can you catch him?' whispered Mummy.

I went over the grass towards him. He threw up his head and looked at me. I went close to him and whispered that he must be good because there was a burglar downstairs. He *was* good. He put his head down and I bridled him, and Mummy gave me a leg up and then ran to open the gate into the field. She looked very funny with the eiderdown flapping.

Cavalier and I went through and Mummy whispered, 'Godspeed.' She wasn't being sloppy, but she was being the watchman in 'How we brought the Good News from Aix to Ghent.'

Cavalier and I trotted along the well-known track and I dug my heels into his sides and he broke into a canter. Soon I saw the stile in front of me and I pulled him up ready to turn into the gate.

If you have any imagination, you can understand what I felt like when I saw that, for the first time since we had come to Hedgers Green, the gate was shut.

I rode up to it. I had never opened a gate from a pony's back before, but I didn't want to dismount because of mounting again. People in books can always vault lightly into the saddle, but it is not so easy when your pony is close on fourteen hands and you are small for your age.

Then, to my horror, I saw that it was no use even dismounting. The gate was padlocked.

I said one of the words that Mummy had said when she was sticking in the window. It was too sickening having my midnight ride spoilt by a silly padlock. I think Cavalier thought so to. He stood still and hung his head dejectedly.

I sat for a minute looking back along the path. There was no sign of Mummy. Our flying hoofs had left her far behind. I looked towards the farm. There was nothing to see but the moonlight on the fields, but far away where the farm was, I heard a cock crowing. I was just going to turn round and go back to meet Mummy when I remembered Young Lochinvar.

I was supposed to know the whole of it, but it was only two lines that I remembered.

'He stayed not for brake and he stopped not for stone,
He swam the Esk river where ford there was none.'

'Come on!' I said to Cavalier, and I swung him round and rode at the stile.

I wasn't a bit frightened until I saw the stile looming up in front of us. I have jumped many bigger jumps since, but somehow none of them have ever loomed as that stile did then. I clutched at Cavalier's mane and I heard myself shout, 'Help!' which I'm sure Paul Revere didn't, or young Lochinvar either, and then we were over and Cavalier was galloping up the slope towards the farm.

I hate to break off where it is exciting, but perhaps you are wondering why a pony that wouldn't jump a bean-pole propped up on two or three bricks, jumped a stile. Uncle Nigel says that it was because I was excited and I 'threw my heart over,' and if you do that, he says, a good horse will have a jolly good try at anything. I know what he means, but I must say it's much easier to throw your heart over when you are capturing a burglar than when you are just trying to win a cup or a silver spoon.

Well, we flew along. The dark hedges with their moon-lit tops rushed by and presently I could see the farm looking fast asleep under its three elms. We clattered into the farmyard, and I slipped off and stood on tip-toe to reach the knocker and banged and banged on the door.

A window was opened above me and a head came out.

'Help!' I said. 'We've got a burglar.' It was a relief not to have to whisper, and I simply yelled.

'If it ain't the young lady from the cottage,' said Farmer Higgins. 'Wait a minute, Missy, till I gets my trousies on.'

It was ages before I heard him clumping downstairs, and he took ages to undo the bolts on the door. But at last he stood there. I said, 'Oh, quick, quick, or he'll be gone.'

Farmer Higgins wasn't quick. He stood staring at me like his own bullocks do. Then he said, 'Where's your Ma?'

I said, 'She's on her way here. We got out of a window and we came.'

Then at last Farmer Higgins did something. He turned round and shouted, 'Fred!' and 'George!'

There were answering shouts of 'Coming, Dad,' from upstairs, and Farmer Higgins's two sons came clattering down. They were grown-up, and they were huge and strong. They had put on boots and trousers, and coats over their pyjama tops like me.

'Burglars at the cottage,' said Farmer Higgins.

Fred, the eldest son, nodded, and they both came out of the house and went to a shed across the yard. Fred wheeled out a motor bike and pedalled it across the yard, and it started and George jumped on behind. The engine roared and spluttered and they were gone.

It had all happened without anyone saying anything.

Farmer Higgins and I listened till the sound of the motor bike died away along the road. Then he said, 'Ah, they're good boys.'

'Do you think they'll catch him?' I enquired.

'They're handy with their fists,' said Farmer Higgins, and he went on, 'Now, Miss, we'll get along and meet your Ma.'

I said, 'Why did you lock the gates, Mr Higgins? I had to jump the stile.'

'Jumped the stile, did you?' said Farmer Higgins. 'Well, I be blowed. I locked the gates because I've got a bull in them fields – brought him home last night. People are funny about bulls and I didn't want no fuss and bother, not at my age. I'll get the key.'

'Oh, don't bother,' I said. 'I like jumping the stile.'

All the same, he got the key and we set off. Just at the stile we met Mummy, walking along very fast under the eiderdown. We explained that Fred and George were speeding on the motor bike along the road, but Mummy said she was afraid that by this time the burglar would be gone.

I felt so disappointed that I dug my heels into Cavalier and we cantered on. Mummy called something after me.

I knew that one of the words was 'wait,' but I didn't want to wait, so I was like Nelson, only I shut my ears instead of my eye.

When I got to the orchard gate I could hear a noise in the cottage. I tied Cavalier to a tree and crept to the back door. It was ajar, and just as I was going into the kitchen, the door between the kitchen and the dining-room was flung open and Fred and George appeared. They had a man between them and they were bundling him along.

'Got him,' said Fred. 'Red-handed. We're going to lock him in the scullery till Dad comes.'

But all I said was, 'Look!' for I'd seen an awful thing.

Shadow was lying stretched out on the stone floor under the kitchen table. In spite of the noise that Fred and George were making, he was lying quite still.

Fred looked where I was pointing and suddenly he took the burglar by the shoulder and began to shake him.

'Now then, what did you give him? Speak up or it'll be the worse for you,' he roared.

The burglar could hardly speak for being shaken. But he gasped out, 'All I give him was a whiff of cloriform.'

'Ah,' said Fred, still shaking him. 'I'd nothing against you till I saw that. But now I know what you deserve. The long drop,' he said, and he shoved the burglar into the scullery and shut and bolted the door.

In case you don't know, 'the long drop' means hanging.

Fred picked up Shadow and carried him out into the air. Then he got a jug from the dresser and filled it at the outside tap and splashed handfuls of water over Shadow's head. That didn't seem to do any good, so he knelt down beside him and moved his paws.

'Artificial respiration,' he said to George.

George said, 'You ought to press on his ribs like as if he was breathing. That's what they did to that fellow what fell in the pond.'

I suppose Fred did it, but I couldn't see because I was crying and of course I hadn't got a handkerchief. George said, 'Now, Missy, don't upset yourself,' and handed me his, which was red with white spots. I dried my eyes and George said, 'Look, he's coming to.'

I looked and I said, 'Shadow,' and he faintly wagged his tail.

Fred said, 'He'll do now,' and he got up. 'I could wring that fellow's neck,' he said.

George said, 'Ar.'

At that moment Mummy and Farmer Higgins came through the gate. We called them into the kitchen and Fred explained how he and George had left the motor bike in the hedge and walked to the house and found the burglar trying to open Daddy's safe, which was in his dressing room. Really there was nothing in the safe but bearer bonds, which are pieces of paper you get to show that you have put money into a company. If you want the money back, you go to the company and show them the bearer bonds, but as a matter of fact these were no use because the company had gone bust. We think that the charwoman, or somebody like that, must have seen that we had a safe and told a friend, and the friend told a friend and that friend told another friend and finally someone told the burglar. Cousin Agnes says that that sort of thing always happens in a village, however nice.

Well, we talked for a bit, and then Mummy went into the hall and telephoned to the police station. They said they would send a policeman for the burglar, and they asked Mummy what he was like. She called Fred to the telephone, and he told them, and they said that the burglar was well known to them, and not just a man who was poor or hungry. All the same, I should have felt sorry for him if it hadn't been for Shadow, who was lying with his head in my lap and still looked limp and ill.

When Mummy came back to the kitchen she brought Sally with her. Sally was still quite a puppy and, because of the carpets, she slept in a big cupboard, that was meant for coats, under the stairs. Sally hadn't bothered about the burglar; she was fast asleep when Mummy went to look at her; but you must remember that she was still quite young. Now that she is grown-up, she is a very good watch-dog, only she bites first and barks afterwards, as our postman knows.

Sally ran up to Shadow and tugged at his ears. He got up and wagged his tail at her and then flopped down again near me.

In the meantime Mummy had lit the primus and put the kettle on to boil. She said that we all felt like a cup of tea. Just as the kettle was boiling we heard the noise of a car, and then there were scrunchy steps on the gravel and a knock on the door. Fred opened it and there stood two policemen. One was an ordinary policeman in a helmet, but the other one had a cap like a chauffeur's or a railway guard's.

Mummy said, 'Good evening, Inspector,' though it was morning really and the cocks were crowing for miles, and she began to explain about the burglar, and Farmer Higgins and Fred and George explained too. The policeman wrote in a notebook and when everyone had finished explaining, he shut it with a snap, and the Inspector said he congratulated us on catching an ugly customer. But I must say I felt rather mean when the burglar was brought out of the scullery and marched away with handcuffs on. We looked so many and he so few.

While Fred and George had been explaining, Mummy had poured out the tea. Everyone had had some, including the burglar. After the policemen and the burglar had gone the Higginses each had another cup and then they got up and we said thank you, and they said, 'Don't name it,' which means don't mention it, and they went away.

I went with George to the orchard gate; Farmer Higgins was going back on the pillion of the motor bike because his legs weren't as young as they were. I took Cavalier's bridle off and gave him six lumps of sugar. Then I went back into the house. Mummy was putting the tea things into the sink. Everything seemed very quiet and dull.

'I wish another burglar would come,' I said to Mummy.

'Oh, Jean, how can you?' she said.

We talked for a bit and then we went up to bed. Mummy made me sleep in her room, and Shadow did too, in case he should feel worse in the night or have a nasty dream. It was ages before I went to sleep, but I didn't wake up till ten next morning, and it was too late then to go to Miss Pringle.

So ended my midnight ride, but there is one thing more to say. In case this makes any of you feel nervous about a burglar coming to your house, please remember that they hardly ever do come – our house was only one out of the millions and millions of houses in England. You must remember, too, that we had a safe that the burglar had heard of, and that Mummy and I were often alone in the house, and probably he had heard of that, too. Of course you may have a safe, but then probably you are not left alone in the house with your mother; and even if you are, the burglar has still got to hear of it, so it is not at all likely that the same thing will happen to you. I am telling you this in case you are nervous, but if you are not and would like a burglar and a midnight ride, I don't want to depress you. I do not think it is at all likely that you will have one, but Daddy says that if you want anything badly enough you always get it, so hope on.

IV

AFTER I had jumped a stile bare-back in the middle of the night, even Mummy couldn't say that it was dangerous for me to jump a bean-pole in the orchard in

MRS BEAZLEY

the middle of the afternoon. I got her to say that I could, and I made a much more solid looking jump out of a piece of wood from the stable partition. I bought a sixpenny pot of paint and I painted it white like the cousins' jumps, but

Cavalier wouldn't jump it: whenever he got near it, he slowed down and stood still. Mrs Beazley, who came to scrub the floors on Tuesdays, *would* come out and try to shoo him over by flicking floor cloths at him and waving her broom, but I felt in my bones that that was a bad way to make a horse jump, besides being undignified. It was rather difficult to say politely to Mrs Beazley that I wished she would leave me alone, so I stopped jumping altogether on Tuesday afternoons.

Then one day when Cavalier had refused eleven times, I had a new idea. I dismounted and ran along with him and we both jumped together. Then I gave him some oats and patted him. I did this several times and then I mounted and he went over like a bird. I never had to run with him again, but I went on giving oats after he had jumped, and I still do, except of course out hunting, or at gymkhanas, when he gets them at the end of a round.

I kept the jump very low until I had got used to it and didn't feel that I could possibly fall off – at first I had just shut my eyes and clung on. Gradually I made it higher and higher. I used to measure it with Mummy's yard measure and I think it was two feet six when the Christmas holidays came. Mummy said that we must ask the cousins to tea and she suggested asking them early so that I would be able to show them that their despised Toastrack could jump after all. I didn't want to show them. I thought that they would think that I jumped badly or that the jump wasn't very high. And I thought that it would be just like

'GRADUALLY I MADE IT HIGHER'

my luck if Cavalier wouldn't jump at all that afternoon. I didn't say anything because I was afraid that Mummy would think me silly, but I hoped – and I prayed in my prayers, too – that it would rain. And it did. It started at half-past nine and it poured all day.

It poured and poured. The cousins arrived in their car and I saw with joy that they hadn't brought any mackintoshes, so I knew that, however tough they were, they wouldn't be able to go out in the orchard and stand in the obliging rain. They all three looked very big and bouncey, and the first thing they said was, 'How's The Toastrack?'

I said, 'Lovely, thank you.'

They laughed and Guy said, 'Mother told us about your burglar. She'd got hold of a story about your jumping a stile on the way to the farm. She must have dreamed it because old Higgins's gates are always open. I can't quite see The Toastrack jumping a stile.'

They all laughed loudly at the idea of The Toastrack jumping a stile.

I felt *furious*. I had to swallow before I could speak, and by the time that I had swallowed they were talking about something else.

'We're going to the meet on Friday,' said Martin.

Guy said, 'When you get a better pony you'll have to hunt too.' I think he was trying to be nice but he didn't succeed.

Camilla said scornfully, 'You might come on foot. People do.'

The gong rang then. It didn't usually, because we made the tea ourselves, but Mrs Beazley had come to help that afternoon. We went into the dining-room and Mummy and Cousin Agnes talked and we ate, and in my imagination I saved the life of a kind old gentleman, and he gave me some riding clothes and a hunting crop with a lash on it, and I went to the meet and was in at the death and the cousins weren't, and the Master said, 'By Gad! that girl can ride.'

After tea the cousins wanted to see The Toastrack, as they would call him though I had told them three times that his name was now Cavalier. I had to get the stable lantern and we went out and ran across the garden in the rain. The cousins shrieked gaily. I followed in gloomy silence.

Camilla opened the door of the loose box and, without waiting for me, barged in.

Cavalier was eating from the manger. He was much fatter, but of course, compared to the cousins' ponies, he was still very thin. I hung up the lantern on a high hook. Somehow I didn't want the shrieking cousins to see his bones.

Guy said, 'Well, he certainly has come on.'

Martin said, 'Do you think so? I think he's still awfully thin.'

'So do I,' said Camilla, 'I think it would have been much kinder to have had him destroyed.' She looked inquisitively round my stable and up at the roof and said, 'Ugh! What an awful cobweb. I hope it doesn't fall on me.'

Before I remembered about being polite to guests, however rude they are, I said, 'I hope it does.'

'Thank you,' said Camilla.

'You might swallow it and die,' I said, 'and then you wouldn't be so keen on having other people destroyed.'

'The Toastrack's not a person,' said Camilla. 'And he'd have picked up by now if he was going to. I shall tell Daddy that he ought to be destroyed.'

'You won't,' I said warningly.

'I will, I will,' said Camilla.

She bounced about and suddenly I forgot everything and I hit out at her. She jumped back and she tripped over Martin's foot and sat down plop in Cavalier's water bucket.

'Ow!' shrieked Camilla.

Guy said, 'It serves you right, you silly little ass,' and he took hold of her and pulled her out of the bucket.

She was *dripping*.

'It's my new skirt,' she whined. 'I shall catch it.'

'Wring it out,' Martin suggested.

'I can't. It's pleats. You'd better flap it.'

Guy and Martin flapped it and then I suggested drying it with the stable lantern. The glass was quite hot and the skirt steamed, but it didn't seem to dry much. 'It's no use. They'll have to find out,' said Camilla.

'I'll say it was my fault,' I suggested.

'It wasn't,' said Guy. 'It was Camilla's. But there's no use in going into all that. They never understand whose fault it is. We'd better just say that she tripped and fell into the bucket.'

'All right,' said everybody.

I took the lantern and we went back to the house. Mummy and Cousin Agnes were sitting by the fire talking about servants.

'So what could I do,' said Cousin Agnes, 'but give her notice?'

'My dear, what *could* you have done?' said Mummy. Then she saw us and said, 'Hullo! You all look very gloomy.'

Guy pushed Camilla forward.

'I've fallen into the stable bucket,' said Camilla, in a little meek voice that I hardly recognised.

'Oh, Camilla,' said Cousin Agnes, 'you're always falling into something. And in your new skirt too,' she said, as Camilla turned round and showed her wet behind.

Camilla looked as though she were going to cry, so I said, 'It was my fault,' though Guy had told me not to.

Camilla said, 'No it wasn't. It was mine.' I thought that was quite decent of her.

Mummy said, 'Oh well, it's a minor tragedy. I expect we can lend Camilla a skirt to go home in,' so Camilla was bustled upstairs and presently she came down in my best skirt, which, though she was a year younger than me, was much too short for her.

'Oh, you do look a sight!' said Martin.

'I can't help it if Jean's so small for her age,' said Camilla.

I had begun to think that she was quite decent, but now I changed my mind again. If you are small for your age, you know how bitter it is to be taunted with it.

50

'I'm glad I'm small for my age,' I said. 'I shall be able to ride in steeplechases.'

'On The Toastrack, I suppose,' said Camilla.

'Girls can't ride in steeplechases,' said Martin.

'They can ride in point-to-points,' said Cousin Agnes; 'and that reminds me, Claire. Would Jean like to join the Pony Club?'

'I'm sure she'd love to,' said Mummy.

I noticed that the cousins looked gloomy, but none of them said anything.

'I'll ask Miss Gosport to send you an entrance form,' said Cousin Agnes. 'It'll be great fun seeing you at the rallies.' She looked at the cousins and said, 'Won't it?' in the voice of a commanding officer.

The cousins said, 'Yes,' meekly, but I knew that it wasn't 'Yes,' that they were thinking.

Soon after that they left. They said it had been lovely, but that was only politeness. When Cousin Agnes said goodbye, she pushed something crackly into my hand, and afterwards I found that it was a ten shilling note. We decided that she meant it for joining the Pony Club.

The entrance form came two days later. I found that it cost half-a-crown to join and that half-a-crown a year was the subscription, so I bought a postal order for five shillings and had four and tenpence halfpenny left, which I spent on Christmas presents. I bought Mummy a rose tree for the garden. It was called Madam Butterfly and it cost two shillings. I bought Daddy some peppermint creams, which he likes; they were a shilling; and I bought Mrs Higgins some caramels, which were sixpence. Then I had one and fourpence halfpenny left for the animals. I bought Sally a scarlet collar, which was sixpence, and Shadow a threepenny bar of chocolate; it was quite fair to spend less on him because he already had a scarlet collar, which had been bought in the days before our family fortunes failed, and had cost six and sixpence because it was real morocco.

Then I had fivepence halfpenny left. Carrots were twopence halfpenny a pound, so I bought Cavalier two pounds. I couldn't find anything for the halfpenny so I gave it to a child in the village.

I must say it was more fun buying presents like that than it had been when I had heaps of money.

The day before Christmas Eve was very dull because Mummy had bought a lot of Christmas cards for me to send to Aunts and Uncles whom I had never seen, or hated, and to people like Mademoiselle, whom I would never see again, thank goodness. I got quite tired of writing 'With love from Jean' and addressing envelopes to places like Bath and Cheltenham, but at last it was done and I rode Cavalier down to the post office and was glad to see the beastly things disappear into the ever open mouth of the pillar box. The next day I went up to my bedroom and locked the door and got out my presents, and wrapped them in tissue paper out of Mummy's hatbox, and tied them up with bits of different coloured wool that was over from my sweaters and stockings. The wool for Mummy's present was blue, and Daddy had brown, which was dull but mannish. The dogs had scarlet and Cavalier a beautiful bright yellow. Though I had hated writing on the Christmas cards, I didn't mind writing on my presents, and I wrote quite long things like 'Wishing you good hunting,' on Shadow's, and 'May you canter on for ever,' on Cavalier's.

I woke up very early on Christmas morning. When we lived in London I had always had a stocking, which was supposed to be filled by Father Christmas, and my presents from people had been put on the breakfast table but not opened till I had finished my breakfast. This year, for a reason that you will guess if you are old enough, I had not hung out my stocking, but when I woke up I did feel round a bit, and there it was, all lovely and heavy and full of exciting lumps as usual. I lit my candle and began unpacking my stocking.

The things in it were much more exciting than usual. There was an apple first, and then a handkerchief like Fred's – red with white spots on it. Then there was a brown horse just like Cavalier and a stile for him to jump, and then there was a mouth organ. I had always wanted a mouth organ but Nurse had never let me have one because of the noise going through her head. I blew a few blasts on the mouth organ and made the brown horse jump the stile and go galloping away over my eiderdown, and then I went on unpacking my stocking.

I found an orange, and a tangerine which I ate, and a

little paper bag full of acid drops, and then, right down in the toe was the best thing of all – the proper tool for picking out horses' hoofs. I was awfully pleased because up to now I had had to use a screwdriver.

I played with my brown horse a bit. First of all he was young and roamed the boundless prairie. Then he was caught and shipped to England in one of my bedroom slippers. The eiderdown, which had been the boundless prairie, became the sea, and it was very rough and the poor colt was sick over the side of my bedroom slipper. At last he reached England, and he was auctioned, but he was looking so miserable from being seasick that no one would offer more than ten pounds for him. The man who bought him was very cruel and made him pull heavy carts and beat and starved him, so an old gentleman bought him out of kindness and gave him to a girl, who fed him up and rode him in the Newmarket Town Plate and won it. As she was riding him back into the paddock, someone offered her a thousand pounds for him but she said, 'No, thank you. I will never part with him.'

When I had finished this game, Bluey said half-past-six, but as I have told you before, I can't rely on him. It might have been seven. So I got up and dressed and went out to the stable with Cavalier's present. It was very dark still, and I had to take the lantern.

I gave Cavalier his present and read out the writing on it. He was very interested when he heard the paper rustling, and he was awfully pleased when he saw the carrots. I gave

'I PICKED OUT HIS HOOFS WITH MY NEW AND PROPER HOOF-PICKER'

him one pound of them and put the other pound into my pockets. Then I picked out his hoofs with my new and proper hoof-picker. He seemed very surprised at having it done so early in the morning.

I hung the hoof-picker tidily up on the hook where I hang the lantern, and then I went back to the house and let Sally out of her cupboard. We unwrapped her collar, but she was so excited that I couldn't put it on for ages – she wriggled so, and squirmed, and danced round me. At last she rolled over and I got it on, and I must say she looked lovely in it.

I couldn't give Shadow his present yet because, since the burglar came, he had slept with Mummy, so I went into the kitchen and lit the primus and put on the kettle. It was just boiling when Mummy appeared in a fur coat and pyjamas.

We wished each other a merry Christmas and then we made the tea and took it up to Daddy.

He sat up in bed and said that he was sorry he hadn't got us any presents. We said it was all right, we hadn't expected any. Then he groped beside the bed and produced two huge parcels.

Mummy's was a chicken coop and mine a pair of jodhpurs.

I was awfully pleased. Your legs get rubbed if you ride for long in shorts and, besides that, you look silly. I cast off my shorts at once and put on my jodhpurs, and Mummy cut off the ticket, which said five-and-elevenpence.

I rushed into my bedroom and got my presents. Daddy

ate one of his peppermint creams and gave one to Mummy. I wouldn't take one because they looked so awfully few now that two had been eaten.

Mummy was awfully pleased with her rose bush. She said I couldn't have thought of anything nicer. She gave me a lovely knife. It has a tool in it for taking stones out of horses' hoofs. I put it at once into the pocket of my jodhpurs.

While Daddy and Mummy got up, I laid breakfast. There was nothing to cook because it was ham, so when Mummy came down, all she had to do was to make the coffee. When I went into the dining-room there was a huge pile of parcels on the table.

Cousin Agnes had sent me a riding stick. It had a crook for opening gates and a silver band with my initials on it. My London Aunt – the one who had given me the Wendy House – had sent me a party frock. It was pink and Londonish. My Cheltenham Aunt had sent me a box of chocolates. They were nearly all hard, but Mrs Beazley and the dogs liked them. My Bath Aunt and my godmother had each sent me ten shillings. Colonel Bingley, whom I couldn't remember, had sent me his usual box of lovely marsh-mallows. My other godmother had sent me some embroidery to do, and the skeins of silk came in very handy for plaiting Cavalier's mane with. Then, to my horror, there were three small parcels from the cousins.

I was horrified because I had only sent them the beastliest of the Christmas cards that Mummy had bought for me.

I was haunted by remorse as I opened the parcels. Guy had given me an electric torch; Martin a wooden cocker spaniel; and Camilla a book about a pony.

'Oh dear,' I said, 'I only sent them Christmas cards with churches on them.'

Daddy said, 'What *does* it matter? Everybody knows that we haven't got any money.'

'Still, I might have sent them a coach and horses,' I said, 'or even a robin.'

After we had been to church, we went back to lunch with the cousins. There was turkey and plum pudding and everything, and lots of crackers. Camilla was sick after lunch so she had to lie down, and the boys and I went out to the stable. Like Cavalier, the ponies had all had Christmas presents, but they were much better presents than I had been able to give him. Blackbird had a lovely day rug, blue with scarlet binding and Guy's initials in scarlet, and Red Knight had a teak bucket, and Hesperus had a new bridle. The cousins were hunting next day, so we groomed the ponies; I did Hesperus, and he wasn't nearly as good as Cavalier. He kicked at me when I was brushing his tail and wouldn't pick up his hoofs when I wanted to clean them, but I must say his coat was lovely and shone like satin when I had finished it off with Guy's silk pocket handkerchief.

Before we went, Cousin Agnes said that of course I must come to the Pony Club rally on the thirty-first of December, so as soon as I got home I started grooming

Cavalier, and when it was dark I took the tack up to the bathroom and cleaned it. I was very excited about the rally and all the next week I was busy grooming Cavalier, but he *would* roll every morning when I put him out in the orchard, and, as the weather was warm and wet, he got very muddy and it was rather disheartening. I got the saddle beautifully shiny and Mummy patched the place where the stuffing was coming out with a piece of flannel that was over from my pyjamas, but I *couldn't* get the stirrups clean; the cousins hadn't used the saddle for ages and they were terribly rusty. The bridle wasn't bad, though the leather of the headband had cracked rather, and one of the reins was all over the teeth marks of the cousins' Sealyham, who had got into the stable and chewed it when he was a puppy.

Well, the day came. It was fine, which was lucky because I had no riding coat, but it was rather cold so I put on a pullover inside my yellow sweater. The saddle and the bridle shone and Cavalier's coat looked better than I had ever seen it; his tail wasn't bald at all now, and his mane was much thicker. Mummy said that we looked very nice and that the horsey people would know how lovely Cavalier would be when he was fatter.

We waved goodbye to Mummy and went slowly along the high road. I had started early because I didn't want to arrive with my pony sweating. We had walked about a mile when I heard the clatter of hoofs behind us and two girls dashed past on three-figure hunters – at least they looked like that to me. The girls wore bowler hats and black coats and buff breeches and proper riding boots, and suddenly I felt awful with no hat and only a sweater and strap shoes. I noticed then that I was cold and that the sky was grey and it looked like rain – it is funny how you don't notice the weather and being cold when you are feeling joyful and excited. I thought of turning back, only I knew that Mummy would ask why, and I wouldn't be able to tell her; if I did, she would be miserable at not being able to buy me the right sort of clothes.

So we jogged miserably along. The three-figure hunters had disappeared from view and Cavalier trotted as though he was tired already. I thought that I shouldn't have minded about my clothes (except the strap shoes) if I had had a faster pony, and I gave Cavalier a whack with my stick and spoke to him crossly. The poor darling was so surprised that he broke into a canter and I was haunted by remorse. I stopped him and gave him some oats out of my pocket.

He was munching the oats and I was hoping that he had forgotten the whack, when I heard the sound of hoofs coming down a side road just in front of us. In a moment a child appeared on a fat brown pony. A lady was leading it. When she saw me, she said in a helpful voice, 'What is the matter, dear? Won't he go?'

I hate people who call you 'dear' the first time that they see you. How do they know that you are dear and not their future enemy?

'He's all right, thanks,' I said coldly.

But all the same she left the other pony and came up to me, saying, 'Shall I lead him?'

I said, 'No, thank you. He's only finishing some oats,' but all the same she took hold of the bridle.

'I'll lead him a little way,' she said brightly.

But at that moment the fat pony, which had been fidgeting, swerved round and trotted briskly back up the side road. The child gave a wail and the helpful lady let go of Cavalier and ran, shrieking out, 'Hold on to the mane, Rosemary!' I dug my heels into Cavalier and we made off at a fast trot and were soon round a corner and out of the sight of the interfering lady.

Soon we came to the white gates of the house where the rally was. It was a large house, and the avenue went through a park with a lake in it. There were a lot of children on ponies riding about and I went towards them.

A lady, who was standing with some others, said, 'You're the new member, aren't you?'

'Yes,' I said.

She said, 'Jean Leslie?' and I said 'Yes,' and she said, 'Well, we shall be starting in a minute. Here are the Cunninghams.' And the cousins came cantering over the grass, looking very superior in their proper riding clothes and on their shiny ponies.

'This is your cousin, isn't it?' said the lady. I found out afterwards that she was Miss Gosport, the Secretary.

Guy said, 'Yes,' and Miss Gosport said, 'And that's the pony you told me about. He's rather poor still, isn't he?

61

But perhaps he'll pick up when the grass comes. Can he jump?'

Before I could say anything, Guy said, 'No. He hasn't an idea. We tried him.'

I expect you will think that it was silly of me not to contradict him. I think that it was most awfully silly, but sometimes, when you are among strangers, who are talking to each other, you can't say things, especially when they are very important and matter awfully. In fact, the more important they are, the more difficult it is to say them. You open your mouth to begin but you wait just too long and then somebody else says something and it is too late, and Daddy says those are the two saddest words in the English language. I don't know if this ever happens to you – perhaps you are too sensible – but it often happens to me, especially at school when the mistress says, 'Now this is a very difficult question and I wonder if anybody knows the answer?' And I do know the answer, but just as I am going to say it, she says, disappointedly, 'No, I thought you wouldn't,' and it is too late again, and at the end of the term my report says, 'Has little ability.'

When Guy said that Cavalier couldn't jump, Miss Gosport said, 'Well, that's a pity,' and she said, 'We'd better start now. There are a few more to come but it's no use waiting for them.' We all followed each other and rode round in a ring, first at a walk, then at a trot, and then at a canter. Cavalier didn't understand what we were doing – how could he, when he had never done it before? – and there was a boy behind me who kept on saying, 'Oh, *do* get on with your old cab horse.' At last I said, 'Cab horse yourself!' and he said, 'Well, anyhow, I don't starve my pony.' I couldn't explain about Cavalier while we were riding round, so I said, 'You're not the manager of the Pony Club,' and that squashed him.

The next thing that we had to do was to canter one by one round the outside of the circle. When my turn came, Cavalier *wouldn't* canter; he kept swerving back towards the other ponies, and Miss Gosport made me fall out of the circle and go and stand by her and Rosemary, who had arrived and was being led about by her mother. The mother, whose name was Mrs Jones, came and chirped to Cavalier as if he was a canary, and said how thin he was and couldn't I give him something fattening? I felt very miserable standing there by the feeble Rosemary while the other children were cantering gaily round and being told how good they were.

When the last one had finished, we all rode into a field where there were jumps arranged as they are at a show or a gymkhana. We all stood about and Miss Gosport called out people's names and they went over the jumps. Cavalier and I stood next to the boy who had made the remark about the cab horse, but he didn't speak to me, nor did any of the other children. But they talked to each other a lot, and I felt very left out, and wished I hadn't come. I thought that they didn't speak to me because they despised me for my thin pony and for not having a riding coat and for my strap shoes. Of course it was very silly of me and

I hope that if, after reading this, any of you go to a Pony Club rally for the first time and nobody speaks to you, you will not make the same mistake as I did. As long as you are keen, people do not mind if you wear strap shoes or even your ordinary winter coat with fur on it. If they don't speak to you it is not because they despise you but because they cannot think of anything to say.

Well, there I sat feeling miserable and despised, while the other children jumped, and I did hope that when the last one had finished Miss Gosport would tell me to have a try, but she didn't. She turned round and said in a kind voice, 'Well, I expect that one day you two little ones will be jumping like that. Won't it be glorious?' and I realised with horror that 'you two little ones' were me and Rosemary. My throat went tight as it does when you are going to cry, and I was afraid that I was, so I turned Cavalier round and without a word rode hastily from the scene of disaster.

I couldn't see where I was going but I suppose that Cavalier knew the way, for, by the time that I had found my handkerchief, we were at the avenue gates. My handkerchief was the one that I had bought with my Christmas money. It had hunting scenes on it, and of course when I saw the people jumping five-barred gates on it, I started to cry again. So I put my handkerchief away and dried my eyes on my woolly gloves and I was only just in time, for, in a moment, I heard a shout behind me, and there were the cousins riding along the grass at the edge of the road.

Guy came up with me first. He said, 'What's the matter? You *did* leave in a hurry.'

'I thought it was finished,' I muttered.

'Well, so it was,' he said, 'but you needn't have gone tearing off like that. How did you like it?'

I said, 'It was lovely.'

Martin and Camilla rode up then, and they both asked me how I had liked it. I said to both of them that it had been lovely.

Guy said, 'You must come round one day and try jumping on our ponies.'

'I don't want Hesperus's mouth jagged, thank you,' said Camilla.

'You jag it enough yourself,' said Martin.

'I don't,' said Camilla.

'You do,' said Martin.

'You pig! You beast! I hate you!' said Camilla.

This argument gave me time to say at last, 'Cavalier *can* jump.'

'Oh good,' said Guy. 'That's splendid. You'll be able to enter for all the gymkhanas.'

It was only afterwards that I realised that he meant this as a joke. He didn't believe that Cavalier could jump, but thought I was just saying it because I was fond of my pony.

I said, 'When are they?'

'In the summer holidays,' said Guy. 'They send you a notice.'

I made him tell me how high the jumps were, and what

they looked like, and he told me about the competitions. Then we came to the crossroads and the cousins went one way and I went the other. After a bit I met Mummy, who had walked with Sally and Shadow to meet me. She said, like the cousins, 'Well, how did you like it?'

I said once again, 'It was lovely.'

She began to ask me questions, which was very awkward, because I didn't want her to know that I had been miserable. I answered, 'I don't know,' to most of them and Mummy got annoyed and said that I didn't seem to know anything. Luckily we were nearly home by then, so I changed the subject by asking what there was for lunch. Mummy said that there was ham and baked potatoes and rhubarb afterwards, so I cheered up and began to forget about the Pony Club.

Before I put Cavalier into the orchard I gave him some oats so that he should forget too, and I am sure that he did, for as soon as I had let him go he dashed off like a three-year-old and rolled madly in his favourite corner under the apple trees.

V

OTHER Pony Club rallies had been arranged for the Christmas holidays, but first of all I had a cold and couldn't go, and then there was a frost and the ground was too hard, and then it rained and I couldn't go because I had no riding coat. I was glad, but I had to pretend that I wasn't, and I found that it is quite as difficult to look disappointed when you are not as it is not to look disappointed when you are. Mummy was very sorry for me and did things like buying me acid drops and letting me have golden syrup instead of jam for tea, and I must say that I felt rather mean.

Owing to my cold and their colds I did not see the cousins again during the Christmas holidays, and soon they had all gone back to school again and I was going to Miss Pringle in the mornings and riding whenever it was fine in the afternoons. Spring began to come, and it was light after tea, and some crocuses came out in the garden and then some daffodils in the orchard, only the gander ate them, so they were soon gone. The hens began to lay at last and then I really did go round and collect eggs in a little basket, only the little basket was generally lost, so I collected them in my pockets and my hands. The goose, whose name was Edith, made a nest behind the orchard gate where the violets grew, and she laid seven eggs and sat on them, looking very sweet with the violets all round her. The gander, whose name was Harold, got very fierce, and he used to chase the dogs away from the nest, and Mrs Beazley too, when she went out to hang up washing or to twirl her mop.

About that time we got a letter from my sentimental aunt saying that she would like to come and stay. If you live in the country I daresay you have noticed that people always want to come and stay with your mother in the spring and summer when the weather is fine; no one ever suggests coming in January or November. I said, 'Oh, please don't have her,' but Daddy and Mummy said that we must because there was no excuse that we could give, and because she had always been so kind. They said, had I forgotten all the lovely presents Aunt Daphne had given me? and certainly they had been very expensive presents, but none of them had been what I wanted. Aunts seldom realise that you would sooner have a sixpenny mouth organ than a three-guinea party frock.

Well, Mummy wrote back that Aunt Daphne could come, and we polished up the spare room, and I arranged a bowl of primroses and catkins for the dressing table, and she came. She came in a new car, and the first thing she said was that she would take me for a drive in it; she was one of those people who think it is a treat for you to be driven along a road in a stuffy old motor car. She left her suitcase at the cottage, and I had to go with her to show her the garage in the village, and we walked back together. We met Mr Perks, and she said she wondered how often he washed, and I said coldly that he was a friend. The next thing she said was that she was dying to see my pets. I *hate* people who call your animals 'pets.' None of ours were 'pets.' They were proper working animals like on a farm.

Well, we had lunch. Mummy had burnt the potatoes rather, and Aunt Daphne looked at them and said she never touched potatoes. For pudding there was jelly, which was one of the few puddings that Mummy and I could make, and she said that she didn't touch jelly, but would like some bread and cheese. I looked in the larder, but, of course, there was no cheese, so she ate bread and butter, and we felt very uncomfortable. After lunch she tried to be unselfish and wanted to wash up, which would have annoyed Mrs Beazley dreadfully because she can't abear strangers in her kitchen. Mummy argued with her, and at last she was persuaded not to, and I took her out into the orchard to look at my 'pets.'

She wouldn't come along at first but stood admiring the apple blossom. I had a carrot for Cavalier, and I went on ahead to give it to him. Suddenly I heard a crack and I turned round and saw that she had reached up and broken off a long bough of apple blossom.

I said, 'Oh!'

'What's the matter?' said Aunt Daphne.

'Well,' I said, 'it would have turned into apples.'

'Oh, but it's much more beautiful like this,' she said, not at all squashed.

Cavalier had seen the carrot in my hand and he came up to me.

'My dear,' said Aunt Daphne, 'what a poor old thin pony.'

I said nothing.

She said, 'I hope you give him lots and lots of bran mashes.'

I said, 'He has one every Sunday.'

'I should give him one every day,' said Aunt Daphne. 'Let's begin today, shall we? I'll buy you the bran. I expect we can get it in the village.' She is the sort of person who is always trying to rescue other people's animals.

'Thank you, but he mustn't have bran mashes every day; it would make his bowels too loose,' I said, like the horse book.

'My dear Jean! Really!' said Aunt Daphne.

She seemed to lose interest in Cavalier after that, so I showed her Edith, sitting among the violets.

'Oh, how sweet,' she said. 'I must stroke her.'

I suppose it was wrong, but I let her trip away towards Edith. She was quite near the nest when Harold saw her.

He gave a loud squawk and flew through the air with his lovely grey wings spread and his yellow webbed feet dangling. He came to the ground a few yards away from Aunt Daphne and taxied like an aeroplane towards her. Then he seized the back of her skirt in his beak and started shaking it.

Aunt Daphne gave a shrill shriek and turned round to see what was happening. She bent down to push Harold away and he spread his wings and beat at her. By this time Edith was squawking too, and the hens were clucking and Aunt Daphne gave another shriek, so the noise was lovely.

I rushed up and said, 'Get away, Harold!' and he ran off towards Edith, stretching his neck and boasting. He is never in the least fierce with either me or Mummy.

Aunt Daphne was looking furious. Harold had hit her on the nose with the tip of his wing and her eyes were watering. She dabbed her eyes with her lace handkerchief and said, 'That bird's dangerous.'

I laughed at the idea of Harold being dangerous. Aunt Daphne thought that I was laughing at her and said, 'Don't be rude. There's nothing to laugh at.'

Then Mummy came rushing out to see what had happened. When we had explained, she said that I was very stupid to let Aunt Daphne try to stroke Edith. I said, 'I thought she knew all about animals.'

'I have never had to do with geese,' said Aunt Daphne haughtily. The fact was that she had never 'had to do' with any animals: she liked rescuing them, but I am sure that she had never mucked out a stable or cut open a crop-bound hen.

Mummy changed the subject by suggesting that she and Aunt Daphne should walk to the farm and I should ride with them, so I caught Cavalier and we all went off together.

Aunt Daphne was very tiresome. She would keep stopping to look for flowers. She knew all their Latin names and tried to teach them to me, and Cavalier and I both got the fidgets waiting about for her. I think she really liked flowers better than animals. Of course, unless they are man-eating orchids from tropical forests, flowers don't peck or kick you. On the other hand you can't be sorry for them, and people like Aunt Daphne like to be sorry for things even if there is no need to be.

The rest of the day was dull, but the next day was exciting – at least, at the time it wasn't exciting: it was awful. Even now I hate to wake up in the night and think of it.

I got up and had breakfast and went to Miss Pringle as usual. It was a fine day, and all the time that I was doing lessons Mary sat on the window ledge among the geraniums and Stanley sang in the shrill unmeaning voice of canaries. Aunt Daphne says that it is cruel to keep canaries in cages, and when I told her about Stanley she said that she was sorry for him, but I have seen a lot of Stanley and I am quite sure that he is happy. He is in fearfully good condition, which he wouldn't be if he was miserable, and he hops about and sings his head off all day long. Sometimes when Miss Pringle was cross with me and I was miserable, I used to find him very unsympathetic.

Miss Pringle was in a very good temper that morning. I told her about Aunt Daphne and kept her off lessons for ever so long. My fractions actually came out right, and everything seemed as merry as possible, and I walked home singing 'Old Faithful,' and thinking of Cavalier. I was turning the last corner when I heard someone whistling, and then I saw Mummy walking very fast and distractedly along the road.

'Oh, Jean,' she said, 'I suppose you haven't seen Sally?'

'No,' I said. 'Why? What's happened?'

Mummy forgot to be grown-up. She said, 'That ass, Daphne, insisted on taking the dogs for a walk and she's lost Sally.'

I went cold all over. I thought of traps and I thought of keepers with guns and I thought of rabbit holes and I thought of a puppy we had heard of that had simply run round and round in the woods and starved to death. I said, 'Where did she walk to?'

'I don't believe the idiot knows,' said Mummy. 'As far as I can make out she went through the fields and down into Bottom Wood, and then she says she went through some more fields and into a wood where it says "Trespassers will be prosecuted." She was picking some bluebells when she realised that Sally was missing, but she doesn't seem to know just when she disappeared. Apparently she didn't look for her much, but meandered on and came back by the highroad. I thought perhaps Sally had tracked her so I came to look.'

I said, 'We'd better find the wood where she picked the bluebells. I'll go on Cavalier.'

'You must have some lunch first,' said Mummy.

I said, 'I don't want to have lunch. I want to find Sally.'

'Don't be silly,' said Mummy. 'No search party ever goes out on an empty stomach. I shall look for Sally too, and your Aunt Daphne can jolly well amuse herself.'

By this time we had reached the cottage and we went in. It made me very miserable to see Sally's basket with no one in it. Shadow welcomed me as usual, but he looked rather subdued. Aunt Daphne did not look at all subdued. She was sitting in the drawing-room humming and looking at a catalogue of hats.

I asked her, 'Which wood were you in?'

'What does the child mean?' said Aunt Daphne to Mummy.

'Where you lost Sally,' I explained.

'I didn't lose her,' said Aunt Daphne. 'She ran away after a bunny rabbit, naughty little girl. Don't worry, darling, she'll come back all right.'

'Not if she's caught in a trap or stuck in a rabbit hole or shot by a keeper,' I said coldly.

'You've too much imagination, darling,' said Aunt Daphne

laughing. Yes, she laughed! She didn't know what a crime it is to lose another person's dog in the country.

Then Mummy said that lunch was ready. I don't know what we had, because I was thinking about Sally, but I know that Aunt Daphne ate a lot – it was all nonsense about her not touching potatoes. I was longing to be off, but she had a second helping and then 'just a spot more of that delicious salad.' I fidgeted so much that at last Mummy was merciful and said that I could go if I liked and not bother about pudding.

I ran out and saddled up Cavalier, and I told him that we were going out to find our darling Sally. He put his head down and nuzzled me, and as soon as we were through the orchard gate he broke into a canter. Though I always tell him everything, I don't believe that horses understand the actual words you say to them, but they know what you are feeling like, and he knew that I was anxious and in a hurry.

We cantered over the fields and I looked alternately for rabbit holes and for Sally. When we got to the farm I rode

'CAVALIER AND I WENT DOWN THE TRACK'

round to the yard and asked Fred, who was loading manure into a cart, if he had seen anything of Sally. He said that he hadn't, but that he would keep his eye open, and so would George and Dad and Mother and Mr Gammon, the cowman. He said that he supposed Aunt Daphne was a lady from London and that he had never thought much of folks from up that way.

Cavalier and I went down the track that leads from the farm into Bottom Wood. I called and whistled as we went. Bottom Wood was looking rather lovely. The big beeches were bare still, but the baby ones that stood among them were green, and in the clearings you could see the new bracken, silver grey and curly, in the tumbled brown of last year's. There were puddles in the track and there were no clouds, so they were blue.

Beechwoods are quite good to look for dogs in because there is no undergrowth. None of the messy things that grow in other woods can grow under beeches, and people who live among them never like other woods that are full of brambles, and bushes where things lurk, and caterpillars. We once went to Epping Forest and it was awful. Brambles tripped us up and caterpillars fell off oak trees on our heads. The only people who do not like beechwoods are people who want to have pheasants.

Cavalier and I went through Bottom Wood whistling and calling. It is a very big wood and it took us about half-an-hour or more to get to the other side. I had never been there before, and I felt quite excited, as you never know what may be waiting for you on the other side of a wood. Actually it was quite dull. There were some fields with pigs in them but no gate, so we turned to our right and rode along a track at the end of the wood till we found a place where the hedge was fairly low and we jumped it. Unfortunately there was a pig lying wallowing in the ditch under the hedge, and it leaped up under Cavalier's hoofs with a loud squeal, and he shied and I fell off and landed just where the pig had been wallowing.

I fell off where I usually do, over Cavalier's shoulder. The ground was quite soft and I wasn't hurt at all, but my clothes were wet and rather piggy. I was glad to see that Cavalier was standing quite still in the middle of the field, looking silly and embarrassed as ponies do when you fall off them.

I remounted, and we rode through the pig field and then through a field with nothing in it, and then we came to a large and gloomy wood and there was a gap in the hedge, and two strands of barbed wire stretched across it, and a notice saying 'Trespassers will be prosecuted.' I wondered if it was the notice that Aunt Daphne had seen, but she hadn't said anything about barbed wire so I was doubtful. Then I saw that some way inside the wood there was a patch of bluebells, so I was certain.

I got off and looked at the barbed wire. It was rusty but good and the posts were quite firm. I wished that I had had the sense to bring wire-nippers, but I hadn't, so it was no use wishing. I looked at the wire again and saw that it was attached to the posts by staples, and that the wood of the posts was damp and mossy. I took out my knife and opened the tool for boring holes.

It is a good strong tool and the staples flicked out sweetly one after another. Then I pulled the wire to one side and led Cavalier into the wood where trespassers were prosecuted.

We rode up to the bluebell patch, whistling and calling. This wasn't a nice wood like Bottom Wood. There were all sorts of trees, thick ones like yews and hollies, and there were brambles and rhododendrons which I heard afterwards had been planted on purpose as cover for the pheasants by the owner of the wood, who was Lord Highmoor. It seemed an awful place to be lost in, and after I had called and whistled for ages and nothing had happened I began to despair.

I despaired for a bit, and then I thought how silly it was when I hadn't looked for Sally for

LOOKING FOR SALLY

more than two hours, so I rode on. The tracks in that wood were all small and brambly and apt to stop, not like the nice

79

big tracks with wheel ruts in Bottom Wood, and several times we had to turn back. After a bit I shouldn't have known which way round I was except for the sun.

An hour passed. I couldn't tell the time by the sun, but I could tell it by my tummy, which said in an uncomfortable way that it was half-past-four, which is tea-time. However, this was no time to think about tea, so we rode on. Suddenly we came out into a ride, and standing in the ride with a gun under his arm was a man who looked like a gamekeeper.

I rode towards him to ask if he had seen Sally, and he walked towards me. When we were near enough I was just going to begin but he spoke first.

'What do you think you're doing in this 'ere wood?' he said crossly. 'Do you know as you're trespassing, Miss? This 'ere's private property. Can't you read, or what do you think them notice boards is for? Plain enough, ain't it – trespassers will be prosecuted?'

He had asked so many questions at once that I couldn't think which to answer, so I said, 'Have you seen a small black cocker spaniel bitch, please?'

He said, 'No, I 'aven't. If I 'ad, I'd 'ave given 'er a taste of this 'ere,' and he patted his gun.

I said, 'Oh, please don't. She wasn't hunting or anything. And it wasn't our fault. My aunt from London took her out for a walk and lost her in this wood and I'm looking for her.'

'That may be so,' said the gamekeeper. 'But you can't

look for no dogs 'ere. This 'ere's private property. Trespassers will be prosecuted. By order of 'is lordship, that is, and 'e's a magistrate. Now you get out of this, Miss, quick sharp, and I means it.'

'What lordship is it?' I asked him.

'Lord 'Ighmoor,' said the gamekeeper.

I tried to look dignified.

'Oh, well, then,' I said, 'there's nothing to bother about. I'll make it right with his lordship. You needn't worry, my man.'

I don't know whether I *did* look dignified, but anyhow it worked. The gamekeeper said, 'Oh, well, if that's how it is . . . But I'd be obliged if you'd keep to the paths, Miss.'

'Of course I will,' I said. '*I'm* not a London person. I know quite well that pheasants mustn't be disturbed. And would you keep your eye open for a small black cocker spaniel bitch, please?'

He said he would, and he showed me which way he was going, and I rode off in the opposite direction. For ages I rode about that wood whistling and calling. The sun went down and I began to feel cold and awfully hungry, and the only consolation was that I was so far from home that no one could call me to come in before I had found Sally. Cavalier began to get tired, and when I wanted him to hurry, because I knew that it would soon be dark and I should *have* to go home, he wouldn't. And, worst of all, my mouth got dryer and dryer until I could hardly whistle.

I was just thinking that I should have to turn home,

and wondering where the bluebell patch and the gap were, when I thought I heard a little noise somewhere to the right of the path that I was following. During that long and awful afternoon I had heard lots of little noises that might have been Sally whining, but had turned out to be trees creaking or cock pheasants calling, and I had seen lots of little black things that might have been Sally lying exhausted, but had turned out to be patches of mud or gaps in the brambles, so that I didn't feel in the least hopeful, but I noticed that Cavalier had pricked his ears and thrown his head up, so I stopped him and we stood and listened. Everything was quiet for a minute and then the little noise came again, and it really did sound like Sally yapping. It seemed to come from behind some rhododendrons, so I slipped off Cavalier and buckled the reins round the branch of a tree and went crashing through the brambles.

The rhododendrons were very thick, but I pushed my way through them, and there, on the other side of them was a rickety iron railing running round the top of a chalk quarry. I am an *awful* coward about heights. I *hate* places like Beachy Head and I *quake* when Aunts or Uncles say, 'Take my hand, dear, and look over,' so I went very gingerly towards the edge and held on to the railing and called, 'Sally!' From far below came a little yap and from behind the rhododendrons Cavalier whinneyed hopefully.

For a minute I couldn't think what to do. In books, when things fall down cliffs you run for the coastguard, or you are frightfully brave and climb down, cutting hand-holds with your clasp knife. I thought of both of those things, but the first was no use because I wasn't by the sea so there was no coastguard, and the second was no use because I am not frightfully brave but only ordinary. Then I remembered that, of course, there is always a way into quarries where carts go to get the chalk, or whatever it is, at the bottom. I looked over a bit more and could see the way in, though I still couldn't see Sally.

I ran back to Cavalier and rode him down through the wood and turned to the right towards the quarry. Soon we struck a path with wheel ruts in it, and in another minute we were in the quarry. I *hated* going in because I was afraid that I should find Sally bleeding to death or with all her legs broken, but instead of either of those awful sights I saw what for a moment seemed worse – nothing.

Cavalier stopped of his own accord, and I called, 'Sally!' There was a hateful echo and it went on calling, 'Sally!'

I heard nothing for a minute except the beastly echo and then I heard another little yap, and I saw her.

She was on a ledge quite near the bottom of the steepest part of the quarry. It was a horrid little sloping ledge with grass on it and a tiny thorn bush. Sally was dancing about and squirming and wagging her tail at me and I was terrified that she would fall off, so I didn't call any more but rode up to her. Cavalier had been very good all day, but now he was tiresome. He wouldn't go sideways up to the cliff, but edged away from it. It took me ages to get him to stand just under the ledge, but at last I managed it. Then I stood in my stirrups and held my arms out and called Sally.

She danced and wagged her tail and came right to the edge but she wouldn't jump. Several times she looked as if she was going to, but at the last minute she said, 'Oh dear, I can't face it,' and squirmed away. Then Cavalier got tired of standing and walked off, and I had all the trouble of getting him sideways to the cliff again. Night was falling and I was getting colder every minute, and at last I got cross and shouted, 'Come here!' angrily, in Daddy's voice. Sally jumped at once and I missed her, but I managed to claw the skin of her back as she fell between Cavalier and the cliff. That broke her fall and she slithered quite gently to the ground. I dismounted and picked her up in my arms.

She was awfully pleased and licked my face all over, but, as I have said before, night was falling, and this was no time for kissing. I held her under my left arm and tried to mount. It was an awful struggle, but Cavalier stood like a rock and at last I managed it.

I sat back in the saddle and put Sally in front of me. It was terribly uncomfortable; her legs kept slithering on the saddle and I couldn't hold her with one hand, so I knotted the reins and rode Cavalier with my heels and knees. It wasn't at all difficult, not because I am a good horsewoman but because Cavalier is so handy. Sometimes I think he must have been trained as a polo pony.

We rode through the dark wood in what I hoped was the direction of the bluebell patch, but I couldn't be clever about the way because there was no sun, only one star shining. One of my uncles, who is the sort of person who likes instructing you, had told me a lot about the stars once, but I hadn't listened, and I must say, as time passed and still we didn't come to the bluebell patch, I was sorry. Other stars came out and I suppose my instructive uncle could have found his way quite easily, but they looked a muddle to me, and presently I had to admit to myself that I was alone and lost in that huge dark wood.

I said, 'Go home,' to Cavalier, and stopped guiding him with my knees. If he had been a pony in a book he would have taken me home, of course, but, being a real pony, he just stood still and began to eat brambles. I rode on, and suddenly I saw that there were no more trees ahead of me but rising ground with dark shapes on it, which must be gorse bushes, and above the ridge the sky, blazing with stars. I rode towards the ridge and then I saw a broad beam of light swinging over it, and I knew that the light was a car's headlamps, and that I was coming out on the high road where it crosses the common on the cousins' side of the village of Hedgers Green.

When we reached the road and all our adventures were over, Cavalier suddenly made up his mind to be helpful. He swung round to the right and set off at a brisk trot before I could stop him. I nearly fell off when he swerved, and then I grabbed at the reins and nearly dropped Sally.

The car, which was coming towards me, stopped and a man jumped out and shouted 'Whoa,' and 'Steady.' I thought he might be a bandit or a kidnapper until I saw by the light of the headlamps that it was only Daddy.

'Hullo,' I said. 'I've found Sally.'

Grown-ups *are* funny. He didn't say anything about Sally. He said, 'Oh, Jean, you *did* give us a fright. We've all been out looking for you.'

'What on earth for?' I said. 'Mummy knew that I was looking for Sally.'

'We thought you might have had a fall,' he said. 'The pony might have put his foot into a rabbit hole. Give me that dog and I'll go on ahead and tell your mother.'

He put Sally into the car and drove on. It was lovely not having her slithering about on the saddle. We walked down the hill and then we clattered like a troop of Prince Rupert's Horse through the silent village.

When we got to the cottage, Daddy and Mummy rushed out and helped me unsaddle. They said that I ought to have come back before it got dark, but I explained that that was when I found Sally. I told them about the ledge and they agreed with me that she must have fallen from the top and that she might have starved to death there.

I ate an enormous supper of eggs and bacon. When I said good-night to Daddy, he said, 'Well, you're a persevering little bloke, anyhow.' I felt pleased with that because he generally says that I am an idiot. When I said good-night to Aunt Daphne she said, 'I'm sorry I lost

the dog, but I really didn't know you were such fusspots.'
When I said good-night to Shadow he gave me a paw
and said, 'But for you, I should have been a lonely
widower.' When I said good-night to Sally she said
nothing, but snored in her basket.

Mummy said the best thing of all. She said that
tomorrow I needn't go to Miss Pringle.

'TRAINED AS A POLO PONY'

VI

WHEN Aunt Daphne had gone back to London, we began to think about the Easter Holidays. I don't believe that I was looking forward to them much that year. It would be nice, of course, to have no lessons but, on the other hand, Miss Pringle wasn't bad, and holidays for me meant holidays for the cousins and Pony Club rallies and being a 'little one' with Rosemary. I must say I spent a lot of time dreading the Pony Club rallies, which was silly of me, because who can tell what the future may hold?

The future held German measles. Nobody knew how I got them. Daddy said I got them buying Easter eggs for the dogs in Melchester; and Mummy said I got them the day that he took the car when she wanted it, and I had to go in to the dentist by the country bus. Miss Pringle said that I got it giving some undeserving village children rides on Cavalier; and Mrs Beazley said that I got it from leaving my combinations off before the end of May. Anyhow, I went to bed for a few days, which was annoying, because some chicks hatched out and I couldn't see them, and then I got up and was allowed out, but not near other children.

It is rather nice to feel quite well and yet to be infectious. The cousins never came near me, and when Mrs Jones came to call in white kid gloves and asked if I would go to tea with Rosemary, Mummy didn't have to invent an excuse; she just said that I had German measles and Mrs Jones rushed out of the drawing-room and leaped into her car and drove away at fifty. I spent the time making jumps and whitewashing them. I made a stile, and I made a bush jump with some gorse that Mr Perks kindly cut for me on the common, and I made my old jump into a proper adjustable bar. I also made a wall out of an old chicken-house door, which was lying about, and some wall paper, imitating bathroom tiles, which I found in the attic cupboard. I am not a very good carpenter and the stile used to fall down a good deal, but one day when Fred Higgins came with Cavalier's straw he put it up with some long nails that he kept with a lot of other useful things in his pockets, and after that I never had any more trouble with it until that idiot Rosemary came to tea and tried to climb over it and broke the bar.

Of course Rosemary did not come to tea till long after I was out of quarantine for German measles. She came on her fat pony, which her mother led always. He was quite a nice pony – a pure-bred dark bay Dartmoor with a dear dish face and a mealy nose. His name was Bundle. I asked if I might ride him in the orchard and Mrs Jones said yes and Rosemary said no, but Mrs Jones won. She was awfully fussy and insisted on running beside me, puffing and panting and lurching about in her fashionable shoes. At last I got Bundle into a canter and left her behind.

I must say he was frightfully naughty, but what could you expect when he was never allowed to go faster than Mrs Jones? He bucked all round the orchard, but presently he calmed down and I tried him over the bar. He refused, of course, and I shot over his head, and Mrs Jones came running up, flapping like a hen and calling out, 'Are you hurt, darling?' I had got the giggles and my mouth was full of earth and grass so I couldn't answer, and Mrs Jones thought I was speechless with agony, and shrieked to Mummy, 'Fetch some water! Fetch some brandy! Telephone for Doctor Nash!' Mummy kept quite calm and said, 'What's the matter, Jean?' and I said, 'Nothing. It was so awfully funny, that's all.' Mrs Jones said that it wasn't funny and that you never knew what internal injuries you might get from a fall. She went on telling Mummy about children who had got internal injuries while I caught Bundle, which Rosemary hadn't had the sense to do. They were so deep in their chat that I managed to get Bundle over the bush before they noticed, but Mrs Jones's stories had unnerved Mummy and she said that that was enough jumping for this afternoon.

I may as well tell you now that a few months later Rosemary was given a fairy bicycle and after that she wouldn't ride Bundle because she preferred bicycling, so he was sold to a nice girl called Jill. Jill is very young but she is very sporting and she has got him to jump two-foot-six. Rosemary goes about on her horrid soulless little bicycle, and if you say anything to her about riding she says, 'Bicycles don't buck.' I expect she will soon get run over.

'HE REFUSED OF COURSE, AND I SHOT OVER HIS HEAD'

At the end of May something exciting happened which I really must mention, though it hadn't anything to do with Cavalier. Sally had puppies, four of them, all black with little white waistcoats like Shadow's. Two were dog puppies and two were bitches, and I named them Rough and Tumble and Spick and Span. Of course those were only their kennel names. I did not give them proper names because we did not mean to keep them, but to sell them when they were old enough to good homes or as working dogs to keepers.

I tried not to get too fond of the puppies, but they *were* sweet and I couldn't help loving them. Of course their names turned out all wrong. Rough and Tumble were quiet, good little dogs, and Spick and Span were *awful* – as soon as they were old enough to chew they chewed their box up, and as soon as they could yap they yapped without ceasing. They bullied Rough and Tumble and they got out of their box and couldn't get back, and they puddled in their water and dug up the bricks on the floor of the old harness room where they lived. One of the worst things they did was to pull down Cavalier's halter from its peg and gnaw it to bits. Rough and Tumble helped with that, but I am sure they would never have thought of it if Spick or Span hadn't suggested it. We decided that Spick and Span would have to be working dogs and the good homes could have Rough and Tumble.

Cavalier was rather jealous of the puppies but he was very good and never stepped on them when they squirmed round his hoofs in the orchard. The orchard grass was lovely now and he had got quite fat; you couldn't even see his ribs, much less the poverty marks on his hindquarters. His summer coat was a lovely dark bay; Daddy said it was like the mahogany sideboard we used to have in London; and when I groomed him and finished him off with a duster, he shone like a ripe horse chestnut. But he did not get all the grooming that he ought to have had, because I had more to do now. The puppies got naughtier every day and I had to look after them.

One of the most sickening things in life is that summer passes so quickly. There are just as many days in June as there are in November, but you would never think so. June went like a flash of lightning and almost before I could turn round July was going too, and everybody began to talk about the summer holidays. My Cheltenham aunt wrote and suggested that Mummy and I should go to Bournemouth with her and she should pay for us. I *begged* Mummy to refuse and after a bit she did, though she said that Aunt Maud would be offended for ever. A day or two later, when we were at breakfast, the schedule of our Pony Club gymkhana came, and the date was just when we should have been at Bournemouth, walking along a promenade and missing it!

Mummy and I forgot to eat and looked at the gymkhana schedule. Mummy said that I was too inexperienced to do much, but she thought I might go in for one or two of the competitions. There was a riding class and musical chairs and a costume race and an apple-and-bucket race and a bending race and a handy-hunter competition. Then of course there was jumping. In the first jumping class the maximum height of the jumps was two-foot-six, but you had to be ten years old or under. Mummy said she would have let me go in for that but I was nearly twelve, so I couldn't. I said why couldn't I go in for the under fourteen jumping, but Mummy said the jumps would be much too high and I should fall off and break my neck, or make a fool of myself somehow. And she said that I shouldn't enter for anything if I argued.

I was awfully disappointed about the jumping but I had to stop arguing. We decided that I should go in for all the competitions except the riding class – because I couldn't ride well enough – and the handy-hunter competition – because I had no partner. The entrance fee was half-a-crown for each event and it all came to ten shillings.

When Daddy came home and was asked to write a cheque, he said that it was a waste of money. My heart sank, but Mummy said that I had looked after the hens and washed up and not broken much, and that I deserved my wages. So Daddy wrote the cheque and it was lovely filling up the form and putting in Cavalier's name and age and colour.

The next day I put some sticks up in the orchard and began to practice bending. It was a Saturday and Daddy was at home, and the sticks turned out to be his bean sticks. Some of them had broken when I had pushed them into the ground, and he was cross and said look how that pony had cut up the orchard. I explained how awful the grass would have been without Cavalier to eat it and how good it is for pasture to be trampled on by hoofs, but he said he had known that before I was born and that it would be cheaper to have the orchard scythed than to keep Cavalier to eat it. I mentioned the price of stable manure – this is

PRACTISING BENDING

always a good argument when people are telling you what your pony costs them – and then Daddy laughed and went away saying I was a contentious woman. But he took his bean sticks with him.

I went to look for something else that would do, and I found the clothes props, but, just as I was taking them, Mrs Beazley came out and said what on earth was I thinking of? I said I was thinking of bending, but she said that, bending or no bending, she must hang out her washing. I said that washing or no washing I must practise bending, and we were struggling over one of the clothes props when Mummy came out. I let go of the clothes prop and

Mrs Beazley sat down hard and suddenly. Mummy was awfully cross and said that if she had known she wouldn't have let me do anything in the gymkhana, and Mrs Beazley was awfully cross too, and she said that she might have been an invalid for life and that she would tell her husband and he would tell his solicitor.

I left Mummy to pacify Mrs Beazley and I went back to Cavalier. I couldn't bend now that I had nothing to bend round, and I began to feel rather gloomy about the gymkhana. I thought of practising the apple-and-bucket, but everybody was in such a bad mood that I didn't dare get my hair wet, and there was only a week now to prac-

.. WITH STICKS IN THE ORCHARD.

tise in, and we hadn't practised anything but jumping, and that was the one thing we weren't allowed to go in for. I put the bar higher than I had ever had it and I mounted Cavalier and we went over it. I couldn't measure it because I had already lost two of Mummy's yard measures and, when she had bought the third one, she had forbidden me to touch it, but I felt sure that we had cleared three-foot-eight. It did seem hard that we couldn't go in for the jumping.

The thought of the jumping haunted me. I thought about it in bed; and at Miss Pringle's, when I was supposed to be doing fractions, I drew pictures of Cavalier clearing immense obstacles. I felt sure that we should do better at jumping than at the competitions that we had never practised. I did practise the apple-and-bucket, but I wasn't very good at my part of it. I thought my mouth was too small, but I have noticed since that it is children with sticking-out teeth who generally win it.

Well, I kept on thinking about the jumping and then one day when I happened to be looking at the schedule I saw that you could enter on the morning of the gymkhana if you paid a double entrance fee of five shillings. Daddy was always saying that I lacked determination, and suddenly it occurred to me that this would be a good chance to show that I was a determined character. I thought that if I could somehow get five shillings I would enter secretly on the morning of the gymkhana.

I went about looking for five shillings. In London I had known a boy who once found a shilling on the pavement, and, as I went to Miss Pringle's for the last time, I looked along the road and in the grass, and when Mummy came to meet me she said why did I walk with my head down? I looked in the attic cupboards, and in the space under the roof, and in the cellar, but of course I never found anything, and now it was only two days before the gymkhana.

I must say that on that Monday, as the hours passed, I felt very despairing, but I kept on telling myself that it is always darkest before dawn, like it was when I found Sally. It really didn't seem at all likely now that I should find five shillings, and I thought about all the money I had spent in my life on things I didn't really want, like sweets, and plush dogs whose legs broke off, and musical instruments that I left in the garden to perish. On Monday evening I was hanging on the gate wishing that I'd had a saving nature, when I heard the sound of a horse's hoofs, and Guy came riding down the road on Blackbird.

He said, 'Hullo.'

I said, 'Hullo,' and he said, 'How's The Toastrack?'

I said, 'He's all right,' and Guy said, 'I hear you've entered for the gymkhana.'

I said, 'Yes,' and then suddenly an idea came to me. Before I had time to think that I had better not say it, I said, 'Have you got five shillings?'

Guy said, 'Not on me.'

I asked, 'Have you got it at home?' and he said, 'Yes. I've just had a birthday. I've got seventeen-and-sixpence.'

I said, 'Well, can you lend me five shillings?'

Guy looked very surprised. 'What for?' he said, suspiciously.

I said, 'Something.'

'Well, I suppose I could,' he said doubtfully.

'On note of hand alone?' I said. I didn't know what, that

meant, but I had seen it in a moneylender's advertisement in the newspaper.

'I don't want a note of hand,' said Guy, patting Blackbird, who was fidgeting. 'After all,' he said, 'blood is thicker than water.'

'I'll pay you back,' I said, 'after my birthday on the 15th of September. My Cheltenham aunt always sends me ten shillings, so I can offer you a high rate of interest.'

'I don't want any beastly interest,' said Guy. 'I'm delighted to oblige you. I only wondered what you wanted it for. You're not running away from home or anything?'

'Of course not,' I said indignantly.

'All right,' said Guy. 'As long as it's nothing silly. When do you want it?'

'To-morrow will do,' I told him.

'O.K.' he said. 'Blackbird wants some road work so I'll bring it over. Is it secret?'

'Very,' I said. 'Please don't tell any grown-ups or Camilla.'

Guy promised that he wouldn't and then he rode away. At first I was awfully pleased at having got my five shillings and then I thought how awful it would be if my Cheltenham aunt forgot my birthday or sent me a work-basket instead of the usual ten shillings. The thought preyed on my mind and in my imagination I could see my aunt in her drawing-room, which is all glittery with brass ornaments from India and silver bowls presented by grateful regiments, saying to my uncle, 'I think that as dear Charles is ruined I will send Jean something useful this year.'

'I HEAR YOU HAVE ENTERED FOR THE GYMKHANA'

And my uncle, who is a general, but not fierce as you'd expect, replied, 'Just as you like, dear.' I felt fearfully worried, but just as I was going to bed I remembered that boys generally forget things, and, though I had been so fearfully keen to enter for the jumping, I actually hoped now that Guy would forget his promise.

All the next morning I waited about in case he came, and Mummy said why on earth didn't I settle down to something? It was nearly lunch time and I had made up my mind that he *had* forgotten when I heard hoofs coming down the road. I was in the bathroom washing and I rushed downstairs and out into the road.

Guy rode up and handed me a small sack of oats which he was carrying.

'Some oats for The Toastrack,' he said, and then he handed me the sack and with it two half-crowns, which clinked in my hand.

'Oh, thank you,' I said, forgetting how I had worried and only thinking of the jumping.

'Please don't mention it. I'm always glad to oblige a friend,' said Guy politely, and he rode away.

Unfortunately Mummy was in the garden. As I went in she said, 'I thought you hated your cousins.'

I said, 'I don't hate Guy.'

'You did,' said Mummy accusingly, and she said that it was very stupid the way I took objections to people and then had to change my mind. Grown-ups never do realise how difficult it is to know what people are really like.

What happens is that you take an objection to a person because she has corkscrew curls, and you think that she must spend all her time looking in the mirror or sitting indoors sewing and keeping clean, and then, after a bit, you discover that the corkscrew curls are nothing to do with her, but are the fault of her mother or her nurse. Or you may dislike someone because he always wins things: you think he is superior and snobbish, and then you discover that he isn't at all, but used to fall off as much as you do, or else you start winning things yourself and find out that it doesn't make you a bit different and is mostly luck or practise or having a good pony. It is really very difficult to know who will end up as your friends.

Well, I put the five shillings in the pocket of my jodhpurs, after having tied it up in a handkerchief so that it wouldn't jingle or leap out when I ran. Then I went down to lunch. I thought a lot about the jumping, and I began to have the needle – that awful feeling you get before gymkhanas or exams. I had never had it before, and at first I couldn't think what it was; I had pricklings all over me and felt empty even when I had eaten a huge plateful of Irish stew. After lunch I went out and jumped Cavalier. He did a clear round of my jumps, and I thought that was enough, as I didn't want him to get stale, so then we went for a short ride up to the farm. I saw Fred and George and we had a talk about the gymkhana and they said that they were coming to see me win. I felt awful after that and had the needle worse than ever all the way home.

'I GROOMED CAVALIER AND MADE HIM LOOK LOVELY'

When I got home I groomed Cavalier and made him lovely and then I went up to the bathroom and cleaned all my tack. After tea I took the puppies into the orchard and forgot the gymkhana, but when I went to bed I couldn't sleep for imagining how lovely it would be if we won something and I had a red rosette or a blue one or even a yellow one to tie on my bridle. Needless to say I also imagined how awful it would be if Cavalier got one of his obstinate fits and refused to do anything, or if I fell off and everybody laughed and said, '*She* can't ride. What on earth did she enter for?' I made up my mind that whatever awful thing happened I wouldn't cry like I did that day at the rally, no, not even if people called Cavalier a cab horse or if I fell on my head (like I did the day I rode Hesperus), and the St John Ambulance men rushed out of the little tent where they wait so ghoulishly, and carried me on a stretcher from the ring.

I was still awake when Mummy let out the dogs, and still awake when Daddy came thumping up to bed. The last time I looked at Bluey, he said 12 o'clock, and I was awake for ages after then. But at last I went to sleep and, although I had set Bluey's alarm for half-past six, I didn't wake up until the breakfast bell rang.

It was rather awful because I had such a lot to do that morning. I scrambled into my clothes, wondering whether Bluey had gone off and I hadn't heard him or whether he had failed me as he had done several times since his fall. As a matter of fact he went off punctually at half-past eight that evening when it was all over, so I expect I had set him wrong.

I had to rush that morning. The puppies had to be exercised and the chickens fed because we were going to be out all the afternoon. I had a tiresome bantam sitting – I hadn't meant her to sit because it was so late in the summer – and I thought she would never finish her dinner. She went on drinking for ages in irritating little sips and I hadn't yet got a real shine on Cavalier. At last she went back to her box and I shut her up, and Cavalier was looking lovely when the lunch bell rang.

It was awful to think that it was lunch time – half-past twelve, and the gymkhana would start at two. I felt frightfully sick, but I could eat lots; it wasn't the same feeling as when you are ill. Mummy asked if I was excited and I said 'No,' because excited is a nice feeling that you have before your birthday or Christmas, and this wasn't a nice feeling at all.

Well, time went on as it always does, however much you wish it wouldn't, and I finished my pudding, which was treacle tart and very nice, and I went upstairs to change. You couldn't really call it changing, for the only riding clothes I had were my jodhpurs. At the end of the Easter holidays I had had to have a new pair of shoes, and I had persuaded Mummy to let me have lace-up ones instead of the strap kind, so I didn't feel quite so silly as I had felt when I went to the rally, but I did wish that I had a riding coat and a crash cap or a bowler. However, this was no time for wishing, so I washed my face and brushed my hair and ran down to get Cavalier ready.

Of course I had caught him and put him in his box in the morning before I had groomed him, and now I had only to saddle and bridle him. Everything went wrong. First of all I lost the bridle, at least I couldn't remember where I had put it after cleaning it the night before. I *screamed* to Mummy and both she and Mrs Beazley rushed about the house looking for it while I put the saddle on. Since Cavalier had got fatter, my girths were rather short and lately it had been a bit of a job to get them to buckle. To-day it was *awful*. Every time I tried to pull them through the buckles they slipped out of my fingers. The awful thought came to me that Cavalier had got fatter in the night, and that it wasn't possible for *anyone* to buckle them, but it must have been only that my fingers were clumsy from being excited, for just as I was feeling quite desperate, they *did* buckle. Then Mummy came flying out of the house with the bridle, which Mrs Beazley had found in the spare bedroom. Of course I remembered at once that I had put it there because Daddy splashes in the bath.

Even now my troubles were not over. Cavalier had got bored while I fumbled with his girths and now he had made up his mind to be tiresome. As soon as he saw the bridle he put his head up high where he knows I can't reach it, and made an awful face with his lips and looked just like a camel. I dragged in the box, which I use when I am grooming the high parts of him, but still I couldn't reach, and I *shrieked* for Mummy. She *flew* back, but just as she came into the stable Cavalier put his head down and I slipped the bridle on easily.

In another minute I was off, five minutes late and feeling hot and bothered. In all the flurry I had got rid of the needle, but other awful feelings had come instead of it. First, my stirrups seemed too long. I pulled them up and then they seemed too short, so I let them down again. Then I got an awful idea that Cavalier was going lame; his trot seemed awfully funny. I got off and looked to see if there was a stone in any of his shoes, but of course there wasn't. Then I imagined that as he trotted I could hear him breathing, and I thought that perhaps I had let him get too fat, and should break his wind riding him in the gymkhana. I pulled up and went on slowly, wondering if I had better scratch, till suddenly, long before I expected it, I saw flags and tents and we had arrived at the gymkhana.

I forgot all about stirrups and lameness and broken wind, and I dug my heels into Cavalier and we rode briskly on till we came to a gateway. Some children on smart stabled ponies were going in. They looked very professional and wore black coats and bowlers. I followed them at a respectful distance and saw them tying their ponies up, beside others, to a railing at the far side of the field, in the shade of some chestnuts. I rode over and tied Cavalier up too.

The children were putting lovely rugs, with initials in the corners, over their ponies, and I did wish I had one for Cavalier. However sternly I saved up, it would be ages before I could afford one. There was Guy to pay back and I also wanted a martingale. However, this was no time for wanting things. The other children had finished putting on their rugs and one of them said to the others, 'Come along. We must go to the Secretary's tent and get our numbers.' He was a boy, and, though boys are silly in most ways, they generally know where to get things. So I said very politely, 'I say, could you tell me where to enter for things you haven't entered for?'

He said, 'Yes. In the Secretary's tent. You'll get your numbers there, too.'

'Where is it?' I asked him.

He said, 'We're going there.'

So I went along with them. They were quite nice and asked me what I was going in for. When we got to the Secretary's tent, the boy said to the man there, 'This person wants to make a late entry,' and pushed me forward. I must say, he was a very polite boy.

The man said, 'What do you want to enter for?' and I told him, and gave him the five shillings. It was awful seeing those two half-crowns vanish and not really being sure that I would ever be able to pay it back again.

The man put down my name and Cavalier's. The boy said, 'She wants her number for Musical Chairs too,' and I was given it. The other children got theirs for the Riding Class, and then we all went out of the tent again. There I met Mummy, who had just arrived. She tied on my number and we went to look at the ring. On the way I caught sight of the jumps, which were stacked ready to be carried in. They looked enormous and my needle came on again.

The ring looked very gay. There were cars on two sides of it with people sitting in them, and on the other sides were lines of people not in cars. It was awful to think that all those people would see me fall off.

Well, time went on and the first event started. The children walked round and then trotted round and cantered. I could see the cousins, who must have come when I was in the Secretary's tent; they are the sort of children who never arrive a minute too early. I must say they rode beautifully, though Camilla looked a bit fat, and their ponies looked marvellous. The best children were picked out one by one and put in a row on one side of the judges and the others drew up on the other side. Among the best children were Guy and Camilla and the polite boy.

Each of the best children did a figure of eight, and then the judges talked for a bit and then one of them went forward with the rosettes. He gave the red one, which meant first, to Guy, and the blue one, which meant second, to Camilla, and the yellow one to the polite boy. I looked up his name in the programme and found that it was David Willoughby.

The winners rode round the ring. I didn't look at them because I was feeling so awful – the next event was Musical Chairs, and I had got to ride. My legs felt so weak that I didn't see how I could possibly mount, much less stay on at a canter, and I did wish that Mummy would get nervous and suggest that I should scratch from everything. But she didn't. She only said, 'Guy first and Camilla second! How pleased Agnes must be.' So I said in a quavering voice, 'I'd better go now and get Cavalier.'

Mummy said, 'Yes, do.'

It was quite a long way to the railings where Cavalier was tied, and as soon as I had gone a few steps I thought how awful it would be if I couldn't unbuckle the reins and tighten the girths and get back in time. So I ran and forgot my weak legs, and Cavalier heard me coming and turned round and whinnied. He was all alone now because the other ponies had been in for the Riding Class, and he was eager to be off. I untied him and tightened his girths, and we cantered at his lovely slow canter back to the ring.

Of course there had really been heaps of time. The Hedgers Green Temperance Band was only just getting into its place and chairs were still being arranged in the middle of the ring.

The cousins rode up to me. Blackbird and Hesperus in their rosettes looked very grand. Guy said, 'I shouldn't have known that pony,' and Martin said, 'I wish we'd kept him,' and Camilla said, 'He looks all right but a bit rough. It was sporting of you to enter, for I don't suppose he can do a thing.'

Camilla and I are fated to disagree. I said, 'Why not?'

'Well, he's never been schooled,' said Camilla. 'He was in a milk cart when Daddy bought him. Hesperus was schooled at one of the best places in England.'

'Well, Cavalier was schooled in our orchard,' said I.

'By you, I suppose,' said Camilla, and she laughed contemptuously.

Guy said, 'My dear girl, any fool could ride a perfectly schooled pony,' and Camilla went red and had opened her mouth to answer him when the band struck up a loud hearty tune. We all rode one after another into the ring.

'SCHOOLED AT ONE OF THE BEST PLACES IN ENGLAND'

I was just behind Camilla. In spite of having been schooled at the best place in England, Hesperus was very excited and kicked out every time that he got near the Hedgers Green Temperance Band. I was thinking how much better behaved Cavalier was and what fun it would be if Camilla was out first and Cavalier won, when suddenly I saw that the pony in front of me had swung round and the girl, who was riding it, had dismounted and was rushing towards the chairs. I threw myself off and rushed too, but of course I was much too late. In the chair that I rushed to, Camilla was sitting, and on her face was a smug triumphant smile. I was out first, and I supposed it served me right for having had that spiteful thought about Camilla.

Cavalier and I rode sorrowfully out of the ring while band kept on playing 'Land of Hope and Glory,' which didn't suit our feelings at all. Mummy and Cousin Agnes were at the entrance to the ring, and Mummy said hadn't I heard the music stop? and then I realised that I hadn't, and that Miss

'COUSIN AGNES SAID SOMETHING TACTFUL'

'CAMILLA STAYED IN TO THE END'

Pringle had some excuse for saying that I was the most inattentive child she had come across in forty years of teaching.

Cousin Agnes said something tactful about better luck next time, and I said nothing, but watched the rest of the Musical Chairs, which took ages. Guy and Martin came out quite soon, but Camilla stayed in to the end, and was only just beaten by a girl with plaits, who looked *very* attentive. The next event was the Costume Race. You had to ride from one end of the ring to the other, where a fancy dress for each person was laid on the ground. You had to put the dress on and gallop back, and we were to ride in heats of three.

I was in a heat with Camilla and the girl with plaits, who had won Musical Chairs. As soon as we were started I got in front of Camilla because Hesperus was bucking, but the girl in plaits had got a good start too. We rode neck and neck up to the costumes and I got off and shook mine out. It was a black and white pierrot's dress in two pieces. I scrambled into the trousers and then pulled the jumper on. It was awfully tight and I got stuck in it. I waved my arms wildly and there was a loud crack and the neck split and it went on. Cavalier had stood beautifully in spite of my waving arms, and as I mounted I saw that Camilla was absolutely stuck in the jumper of a Red Indian suit; she was much too fat ever to get it on. As soon as I touched the saddle, Cavalier swerved round and I saw that the girl with plaits had mounted too. She was dressed in a bodice and skirt. We

THE COSTUME RACE

rode back neck and neck, as we had come, and Cavalier laid his ears back and fairly galloped. I did feel proud of him. I wasn't sure who had won, and I didn't like to ask, but the girl with plaits did, and the judges said that I had and that I would have to ride again.

So I stayed by the entrance and watched the next heat to see whom I should have to ride against. Guy and Martin hadn't entered for this race, nor had the Polite Boy. There was a girl with red hair and spectacles, and a girl with corkscrew curls, whom everybody hated, and a boy of about thirteen. Corkscrew Curls couldn't manage her pony, and when the others were struggling into their costumes it was still playing up in the middle of the ring. Red Hair got her spectacles torn off by the Red Indian costume and she was still crawling about looking for them when the boy rode in. I must say I felt sorry for her. I have never had spectacles, but I can guess what a nuisance they must be.

So I had to ride against the boy. I could see before I started that I had got to have the Red Indian suit, and for once in my life I was glad that I am small for my age. I got a better start than the boy and I pulled the trousers on quite quickly, but as soon as I had got that beastly Red Indian jumper over my head I felt sure that I was beaten. I couldn't get my head through the neck or my second arm through the sleeve, and, though I struggled and struggled, nothing split; the beastly thing was far too strongly sewn. I felt absolutely imprisoned and half-suffocated too,

'YOUR PONY GALLOP'

and then the worst happened. I felt a tug at the reins, which were over my arm, and Cavalier began to move. I tore the jumper off, meaning to calm him and then try again, and, as I tugged it over my head, I looked hastily at the boy. I had expected to see him mounted or half-way across the ring, but instead of that he was still struggling with the pierrot costume. He had got the top on but couldn't get the trousers over his feet. I suppose he wasn't good at standing on one leg.

I *shrieked* at Cavalier to stand and had another try at the jumper. This time I was lucky. My head and arms *shot* through. I mounted, and the boy mounted at the same time and the ponies bounded forward together. I must say the boy was much better than me at mounting. I think I mounted from the wrong side; I hadn't got my right foot in the stirrup; I was absolutely on Cavalier's neck, and my reins were all anyhow. I didn't bother about my stirrup but I just shrieked something – I don't know what – to Cavalier, and he laid his ears back again and simply galloped. For a moment we were neck and neck, and then I saw to my joy that Cavalier was drawing ahead. We flashed past the judges and pulled up about ten yards beyond the entrance to the ring. At least I did, because, though Cavalier is a bit hard-mouthed after the milk cart, he is always very obliging. The boy went half-way across the field before he could stop his pony. Then he trotted back, and as he passed he said to me, 'Your pony *can* gallop.'

THE APPLE AND BUCKET RACE

I felt very proud of Cavalier then. My face got hot and I thought it was probably getting red too, so I leaned forward on Cavalier's neck to hide it. No one likes to be seen blushing. His neck was lovely and warm and had that beautiful smell of horse which makes you ache inside when you are away at school and you happen to pass a trades-man's pony.

When my face was all right again I sat up, and I saw the cousins coming towards me. Guy called out, 'Jolly good, Jean,' and Martin said, 'You looked as if you were winning

'A LITTLE SQUEAKY BOY CALLED ANTHONY JOHN'

the Derby.' Camilla said, 'It's all very well for you. You're small, but that Red Indian suit wouldn't go on me. It wasn't fair.' She looked very cross and was making scolding noises at Hesperus.

Guy said in a babyish voice, 'Boo-hoo. It wasn't fair,' and Martin said to me, 'Don't mind her. She wants her bottle.' They do tease Camilla, but I expect it is good for her. It would not be true kindness to let her grow up into the sort of person who, when she doesn't win things, says that her muscles aren't working or that it wasn't fair.

The next event was the Apple and Bucket. My needle had quite gone now and I was enjoying myself awfully. The other children had all become quite friendly – I suppose that they were getting used to me – and somehow I had stopped fussing about being in time or doing the wrong thing. There were three heats in the Apple and Bucket and four people rode each time. The cousins had all entered but not Red Hair, because of her spectacles, or the Polite Boy, because he had a plate that he wasn't allowed to take out even for a minute, or Corkscrew Curls, because her mother was afraid that if she got her hair wet she would have a cold.

In the first heat Martin beat the girl in plaits and the boy whom I had ridden against in the Costume Race and the sister of the Polite Boy. In the second heat Guy beat Camilla and a nearly grown-up boy and the elder of two very pale girls, whom everybody called 'The White Mice.'

I had to ride against the younger White Mouse and the

'THE WHITE MICE RODE VERY CORRECTLY'

Polite Boy's other sister, and a tiny little squeaky boy called Anthony John. You had to ride across the ring to your bucket and dismount, and get the apple out with your teeth and give it to your pony and ride back again.

Anthony John's pony refused to budge, but the rest of us got away together, and we all dismounted at the same time and plumped down on our knees in front of our buckets. My apple was a lovely round rosy one and it bobbed on the water most invitingly. I made a snap at it with my teeth, but they only gnashed together and the apple swam tantalisingly away. So then I tried ferrying it with my nose towards the side of the bucket. I must have sniffed, because suddenly water went up my nose and I started coughing and spluttering. I sat back on my heels to cough, and saw that the White Mouse had got her apple out and was giving it to her pony. Then she mounted neatly and correctly and cantered slowly and correctly home.

The Polite Boy's sister and I went on trying to get our apples till a whistle blew and the judges waved to us. I said to the Polite Boy's sister, 'Can we take our apples?' and she said, 'I should think so,' so we took them out with our hands and gave them to our ponies before we mounted. I couldn't resist taking a bite out of mine before I gave it to Cavalier; it looked so red and juicy. The people in the crowd laughed at me, and the Polite Boy's sister did too.

Martin won the final heat of the Apple and Bucket, so now he had got one first prize, and Guy one, and Camilla

'THE MOST MUTTON-FISTED GIRL I HAVE EVER SEEN'

had two seconds. The girl with plaits had the first for Musical Chairs, but the poor Polite Boy had only a third for riding, and, as he had been so nice to me and had a plate, I did hope that he would win something. He showed me his plate while we were waiting for the Bending, and Red Hair, whose name was Judy, let me try on her spectacles. They made everything look rather fascinating – tiny and far away.

When I saw the posts going up for the Bending I did wish that I had practised it more, and I must say I thought unkindly of Daddy and Mrs Beazley. Guy won the first heat riding against Red Hair, and Camilla won the second, riding against the girl in plaits. Then the Polite Boy beat the elder White Mouse and one of his sisters beat the other White Mouse. The White Mice rode very correctly, but they looked as though they had swallowed pokers, and they couldn't hurry. Then it was my turn to ride against Corkscrew Curls.

Corkscrew Curls had a very lightly-built chestnut pony. He looked as though he would bend beautifully, but though Corkscrew Curls was small and had tiny hands, she was the most mutton-fisted girl I have ever seen riding. She dragged at that poor pony's mouth and did nothing with her knees or her body, and Cavalier won the heat at his calm slow canter. Then Guy beat Camilla and the Polite Boy beat his sister and I had to ride against Guy, and my needle came back as bad as ever.

Blackbird is a very clever pony, but he is much more heavily built than Cavalier – more of a cob – and I did feel that Cavalier would have had a chance if it hadn't been for

125

his rider. So I thought I would leave him alone as far as possible. We had to ride out – between the poles, of course, – and then turn and come back again. I didn't hurry him on the way out, but, as he turned, I gave him a little kick, and at the same time he saw that Blackbird was in front of him. He laid back his ears and simply tore between the poles; though he was racing so, he seemed to know quite well that he must go between them. Blackbird was going beautifully but he hasn't the same kind of dashingness that Cavalier has. Honestly I think that in spite of the milk-cart and everything, Cavalier is the better bred pony, and as Farmer Higgins said to me once, 'A drop of blood is worth a ton of bone.' Anyhow, he beat Blackbird by a short head, and now there was only the Polite Boy to cope with.

As I had won against Guy, I expected to win against the Polite Boy, but you do not always get what you expect, especially in gymkhanas. The Polite Boy had a very smart bay mare, whose name was Melody. His mother is musical and his sisters' ponies have musical names too: one is called Music and the other Gay Tune. Well, we started together and we turned together, and when we were coming back and I saw Cavalier lay his ears back and felt him lengthen his stride under me, I felt sure we were winning. We were actually ahead at the third pole, but as we passed it I touched it with my toe, and it went skew-wiff, and I knew, of course, that we were disqualified. As I pulled Cavalier up I could have kicked myself. It did seem awful that I had let him down when he had been so keen and clever.

'IT DID SEEM AWFUL THAT I HAD LET CAVALIER DOWN'

Still, we were second and I had a blue rosette now to tie on his headband with the red one. I was tying it on when Mummy came up to me. She said, 'You *have* done well. I never expected you to win anything.' I never know what to say when people say things like that, so I just grunted. Then Mummy said, 'Well, you've finished now, but I suppose we shall have to wait for the prize-giving.' I said, 'Good gracious, yes,' and I thought how awful it would have been if I hadn't got a prize and had been made to go home before the jumping. Grown-ups are funny. They will leave the most exciting scenes just to go home to dinner.

For some time I had been too busy to think about the jumping, so now, while the Handy Hunter competition was going on, I began to plan how to get into the ring without being stopped by Mummy. I didn't watch the Handy Hunter at all, and the first thing I knew about it was when Guy and Camilla came out of the ring with furious faces, and Guy said to me, 'Camilla thinks herself perfect and won't listen to anyone. Will you partner me at the next gymkhana?' I was awfully pleased and I said, 'Yes, of course, if you want me to.' I never heard what Camilla had done but she must have messed things up somehow. Although I was too busy thinking to watch, I heard afterwards that the Handy Hunter was won by the two White Mice, who are slow but sure, which, as long as you are not *too* slow, is a good thing to be in that kind of competition.

Well, the White Mice came out of the ring and Mummy was still standing near me, so I muttered something about looking at the jumps and rode off at a canter. Some men had begun to carry the jumps into the ring, but I stayed where I was and kept my eye on Mummy. Presently to my joy I saw her move away from the entrance to the ring and start talking to someone. Taking cover behind some ponies and people I walked Cavalier up near enough to hear my number when it was shouted.

Guy went into the ring first. There was a bush jump and then a stile, and then a bar, and then a wall, and then a pair of hurdles. The bush looked very solid and high and I had never tried Cavalier over such a high wall or hurdles. I thought that the wall would certainly finish us, even if we got over the others.

Blackbird was rather excited and I think Guy had a job to hold him. But he looked as though he meant to jump and he did, till he got to the wall, where he ran out twice and then refused suddenly and Guy shot off and over the wall, and landed on his bowler. He got up and there was an enormous dent in his bowler, but he hadn't let go of the reins, which I am sure I should have. He remounted and rode back grinning.

Martin went in next, and Red Knight touched the brush and knocked off the top bar of the stile. When he came to the wall, he ran out and then refused it, and finally went over. He jumped the bar but refused three times at the hurdles. It was very annoying for Guy and Martin as neither Blackbird nor Red Knight ever refuse anything reasonable when they are out hunting.

The Polite Boy went next. He did a clear round except for knocking the top of the wall off. The eldest White Mouse did a clear round, looking very calm and sitting up as straight as a poker.

Then my number was called. I rode into the ring at a canter because of Mummy.

As I rode in I listened, expecting to hear a shriek of 'Jean,' which I should have to pretend not to hear, like Nelson; but as soon as I saw the tall dark bush jump I forgot all about Mummy. I let Cavalier canter towards it and then, when I thought we were near enough, I collected him, as the books call it, and his ears went forward and I let him go and we were over. We cantered on and went at the stile and the bar in the same way and he jumped them both beautifully. Then I saw that awful wall looming ahead of us. It was only painted plywood, of course, but it did look grim, I must say. Cavalier looked at it and he felt rather doubtful under me, so I sat very tight and pressed hard with my knees as I collected him, and I tried to feel very determined. It had the right effect for I felt him gather himself together and go at it – I expect you know the feeling though I can't describe it properly. He jumped it easily and went on a bit faster than I meant him to, but I let him go and we simply flew over the hurdles. I heard clapping and cheering and I realised that he had done a clear round – the poor thin pony that had been bought out of kindness and called The Toastrack.

'THEN HE TRIED REARING'

I rode out of the ring and patted him madly. Then I saw Mummy.

'Jean?' she said. 'Are you quite potty? You *know* we never entered you for the jumping.'

I said, 'I knew he could do it. I felt it in my bones, and I made a late entry.'

'You did, did you?' said Mummy, and she said, 'Well, you might have told me. I missed your first jump and then I thought it must be your double. And there's another thing. Where did you get the money?'

I said, 'Oh, look, Camilla's jumping.' That was tact. I must say that tact is sometimes very useful.

Mummy said no more but looked at Camilla. I did too. Hesperus was being awful. He danced about for a long time, mostly backwards, and then he tried rearing and then bucking. Camilla stayed on marvellously – I am sure he would have had me off in a minute – and she did get him over the bush and the bar, but when he got to the wall he simply wouldn't do anything. It was difficult to know what was dancing and what was refusing, but presently the judges waved her off and she came cantering back, looking furious. I heard her scolding Hesperus and telling him that he was a beastly bad-mannered pony.

There were only four more people to jump now – the girl with plaits and the younger White Mouse and the Polite Boy's two sisters. Red Hair and Corkscrew Curls and Anthony John weren't jumping because their mothers wouldn't let them, and the nearly grown-up boy was too old, and the boy of thirteen said that his pony wouldn't jump, but everybody said that it was really because he was nervous. Plaits did quite well, but her pony touched the top of the wall and refused once at the hurdles, and the younger White Mouse fell off at the wall – if you could call it falling off; she fell with such dignity that you felt you ought to call it descending. The Polite Boy's sisters each had two refusals. They rode awfully well but I thought their ponies had been oated up too much; they were beautiful ponies but very excitable and difficult. When the last one came out of the ring I had a final and frightful attack of needle. Only the elder White Mouse and I had done clear rounds and I knew that I had got to jump again against her.

It seemed ages before anything happened. The judges stood about fatly, looking at their notebooks. I am sure they would have hurried up a bit if they had known what agony I was in. The elder White Mouse sat calmly on her pony. She looked what books call a formidable adversary. I felt hot and untidy. My slide had fallen out ages ago and my hair was all over my face, and my jersey was out at the back and wouldn't stay in whatever I did to it. My belt had worked up miles above the top of my jodhpurs and it felt very uncomfortable. But the White Mouse looked as if she had just dressed. Her tie was quite straight and her pale hair just showed under her bowler. Her jodhpurs were neither too big nor too small for her – most people's are one or the other – and her socks had stayed up and, though she had a riding coat on and you couldn't see, you

'WE GOT OVER THE BAR'

knew that her blouse, or whatever it was, was tucked in neatly. Her pony was hogged and its tail had been pulled like a hunter's. It really seemed quite impossible that Cavalier and I could beat her.

At last the judges decided to do something. They walked over to the wall and two men carrying bricks followed them. They lifted the wall up and put the bricks under it. Then they went on and put the bar higher. Then they came back to where they had stood before and called the White Mouse's number.

The White Mouse was ready. She trotted into the ring and one of the judges stopped her and said something. It was to explain that she was only to jump the wall and the bar. She put her pony at the wall and he went over perfectly, but when he jumped the bar he just touched it. That was only half a fault and I felt sure I couldn't do better.

The White Mouse rode in. She didn't look either pleased or disappointed. It must be lovely to have a face like that, at any rate for gymkhanas.

My number was called and I rode in, and one of the judges said something. I said, 'What?' It was only to tell me not to jump anything but the wall and bar, which I knew already. Cavalier and I cantered across to the wall and I steadied him and put him at it. He sailed over it. Everyone clapped and I am afraid that Cavalier thinks too much of claps, for he gave a gay little kick-out just for swank, and simply flew on. I had a job to steady him. We got over the bar with something to spare and cantered

'THE SMART PONIES HAD THEIR RUGS PUT ON'

back to the entrance. There was a lot of clapping, and Mummy and Cousin Agnes and Guy and Martin, and even Camilla, rushed up and said things like 'Well done!' and 'Splendid.'

I was awfully pleased that Cavalier had won but it was dreadful to realise that the gymkhana was over.

We talked for a bit and then we rode across the field to the railing and tied up our ponies and loosened their girths, of course. The smart ponies had their rugs put on, and it did seem rather awful that I hadn't one for Cavalier when he had beaten them all in the jumping. Then we went back and stood by the Secretary's tent for the prize-giving.

The prizes were laid out on a table. There were one or two silver cups and there were riding sticks, both hunting crops and switches. There was a pair of yellow riding gloves, and there were books about riding and a martingale and some silver pencils. The prizes were to be given away by a lady whose photograph I had seen in the *Tatler* at the dentist's. The writing under the photograph described her as 'the fastest woman over timber in Leicestershire.' I looked at her with awe and admiration.

Guy got a silver cup for the riding class, and Camilla got a riding switch. She wasn't at all grateful but said that she had four already. The Polite Boy got a silver pencil. Camilla got a book as her second prize for Musical Chairs. I thought it looked nice, but Camilla said she didn't want to stay indoors reading. I was looking at Camilla's book when I heard my name simply roared out and somebody

'THE FASTEST WOMAN OVER TIMBER IN LEICESTERSHIRE'

pushed me forwards. I dropped Camilla's book on the ground and she said, 'Don't throw my prize about,' very crossly. I stooped to pick it up, but somebody gave me another push and there I was at the prize table.

The fastest woman over timber in Leicestershire was holding out a lovely hunting crop and saying that she didn't think my pony needed it, but it would be useful for opening gates with. I took it, and it was so lovely that I nearly forgot to say thank you. In fact I had to turn back to say it and it came out very loud and everyone laughed at me. But nobody sensible minds being laughed at.

While the Apple and Bucket people were getting their prizes I made up my mind to attend and be ready when my name was called for the jumping prize, but I forgot that that there was my second prize for Bending to come first, and I nearly jumped out of my wits when I was called quite soon. The fastest woman over timber handed me the pair of yellow riding gloves and she said rather feebly that she hoped they would fit me. I suppose that by this time she was running out of things to say. It must be very difficult to think of short yet suitable remarks for everyone and I hope that I shall never have to give away prizes. I don't suppose I shall, as I am never likely to be the fastest woman over timber anywhere.

I was pleased with my yellow gloves. All winter I had worn a pair of babyish white woolly ones, the sort you like when you are very young because you think they are like rabbits or lambs. I don't really bother much about clothes, but I had often thought how awful it would be if I was out hacking and met the hounds. I should not dare to follow even a yard in fluffy white gloves. The books say that to wear the wrong clothes when you are riding to hounds is disrespectful to the Master. Now my gloves and my crop would be respectful, whatever my jersey was.

When the prizes for the Handy Hunter had been given, I went up for the jumping prize. It was a silver cup, a lovely fat one on a black stand. I *was* pleased. I gave it to Mummy, because I always drop things, and also because I wanted to clap the White Mouse, who was given a martingale.

'I WAS PLEASED WITH MY
YELLOW GLOVES'

Mummy was pleased too. She kept on saying, 'What will Daddy say?' She was so pleased that she didn't think again about the five shillings, and I hoped that Daddy wouldn't think of it either, but I felt doubtful. Men are more apt to think about paying for things.

Well, Mummy went home in the cousins' car and I rode back on Cavalier. As soon as we were by ourselves I sang songs of triumph to him, mostly out of the 'Lays of Ancient Rome.' The sun was setting over the hills and everything looked very pretty. But I did wish that there was another gymkhana the next day.

When we got home Daddy was already there, but Mummy had been most sporting and had not told him anything. She had hidden the prizes inside her coat when she walked in. I told him all about it and, while I was unsaddling, he went to the 'Dog and Duck' and bought a bottle of wine. It was white wine. I did not like it much but it looked very gay.

I gave Cavalier a huge feed of oats and two cooking apples. I put the cup on the mantelpiece in my bedroom and arranged the gloves and the hunting crop on my chair. They stayed there, looking lovely, for a week, and my clothes went on the floor.

VII

THE morning after the gymkhana was dreadfully dull and everybody seemed rather bad-tempered. The puppies were very naughty. They pulled Mummy's best stockings down from the clothes line and chewed them to ribbons. They were the last of the stockings she had bought in the days when we were rich, but I didn't know that so I laughed, and she was annoyed with me. I didn't go out riding because I thought that Cavalier looked tired, but I think he was really bored; he hung his head over the gate and whinnied whenever I went by. I went by a lot as there didn't seem to be anything to do, so I just wandered about. Then Mummy said that if I couldn't find anything to do she would give me something. That is an awful threat, because if grown-ups find you something to do, it is always something beastly, like tidying your cupboard or shelling peas. I hastened away and soon I thought of something – a fancy dress party in honour of Cavalier.

I couldn't buy anything for my party because I had no money, and, even if I had had any, it would have belonged by law to Guy. But I had three bulls-eyes, so I persuaded Mrs Beazley to let me boil them on the kitchen fire, and I made bulls-eye tea. I also fried some bread for the people who like eating better than drinking, and I got six lumps of sugar out of the dining-room sugar basin, only Mrs Beazley put them back again. However, my bantam (not Flora Macdonald, who scarcely ever lays, but Henrietta Maria) had laid an egg, so I scrambled that, and put everything in the oven to keep hot. Mrs Beazley was rather cross because I had used two saucepans and a frying pan and two basins and a fork and a spoon, so I couldn't do any more cooking, but I had already spent two hours over it, so perhaps that was as well. I told her not to open the oven and went upstairs to see to the fancy dresses.

I expect you can guess who the people at the party were. There was Cavalier and Shadow and Sally and the four puppies and my bantam cock, who is called Charles Edward, and Flora Macdonald and Henrietta Maria, Shadow wore my pyjama jacket and a silly sort of muffler that I had had in London, and Sally wore my pyjama case, which I tied round her with my dressing-gown girdle to look like a skirt. On her top part she wore one of Daddy's coloured handkerchiefs to look like a shawl. The puppies were rather difficult because they were small and squirmed. The girls wore shawls, which were more of Daddy's hand-kerchiefs, and the boys just wore belts off bathing dresses – Mummy's and mine. I took Daddy's bathing wrap, which was made of orange towelling, for Cavalier.

Of course tea came in the middle of dressing-up, but fortunately I had only dressed Shadow, so I undressed him again. After tea, I dressed as an Arab in a blanket off my bed, and I got everybody out into the orchard and then went in to get the food. The bulls-eye tea had gone rather sticky but everything else was all right though rather hard. Mrs Beazley had gone, fortunately, so I was able to take a tray.

I carried everything out into the orchard and, as the people's manners were not very good, I wedged the tray into the fork of a tree. It was a tin tray and it bent rather, but it stayed.

I had got the bantams in a coop. They were not dressed up as it is rather difficult to dress birds. I gave them some crumbs of fried bread and they were very pleased, but I am sorry to say that they did not like their bulls-eye tea. I had the egg, and the dogs and the puppies had fried bread, and so did Cavalier.

We were all eating and making polite conversation when we heard the sound of hoofs. Cavalier threw up his head and trotted towards the hedge. He looked lovely in his orange bathing wrap, but not very dignified, as he was still scrunching. Then I heard shrieks of laughter and I was horrified to see the cousins. They pulled up their horses and shouted to me.

Guy said, 'What on earth's happening here?'

My mouth was full of egg, but I managed to shout back, 'It's a fancy dress party for Cavalier.'

Guy said, 'Can we join in?' and I said, 'All right,' and they opened the gate and came in. I wasn't pleased because I thought they might think my party silly, but they all sat down on the grass and ate the tiny bits of fried bread that were left, and drank the bulls-eye tea. And presently Camilla said, 'You do have fun. We never think of things like this to do.'

I said, 'I should have thought that with three of you you could think of lots of things,' and Camilla said, 'Oh well, boys are no good.'

I thought of Guy and the five shillings and of the Polite Boy, so I said, 'They are worse at most things but better at a few.'

'What things?' asked Camilla.

I said, 'At having money and knowing the way.'

'Thank you for those few kind words,' said Guy. He was feeling in his pockets and he brought out eightpence. 'Let's go down to the village,' he said, 'and get some more food.'

'The shop will be shut now,' said Martin, who always takes the gloomy view.

'You can go round to the back,' I said, 'if you are friends with Mrs Gorsuch, and I am.'

Guy mounted Blackbird and Martin said that I could have Red Knight to save bridling Cavalier. I found Red Knight rather broad and bouncey after Cavalier. Guy held the ponies and I went round to the back with his eightpence as I am friends with Mrs Gorsuch. I bought some chocolate-coated wholemeal biscuits and some bars of chocolate.

Going back I asked Guy if he was getting on all right without his five shillings.

'Of course I am,' said Guy, 'and I know now what you wanted it for. I don't blame you.' And he said that if it wasn't convenient I needn't pay him back till I was twenty-one or earning my own living or married to a millionaire. I may as well tell you now that when my birthday came my Cheltenham aunt did send me ten shillings and I paid him then.

When we got back we found that Camilla and Martin had dressed Hesperus up in rhubarb leaves. I don't know what he was supposed to be. We sat down and went on eating. Camilla said, 'Let's have a party like this at home and Jean can bring Cavalier.'

'It wouldn't be so much fun at home,' said Martin, 'Mummy would buy us things to eat. We couldn't cook things. Probably Watkins would bring it out on a silver tray.'

'That's the worst of being rich,' I said. 'Nothing's any fun. But I'll tell you what. Why not have a dogs' gymkhana? I could bring six, if you can have it soon. And we could use your jumps, and have a schedule, and prizes of food and things.'

The cousins said, 'Yes, let's,' and Camilla said, 'Oh, Jean, you do think of lovely things.'

We decided to meet secretly next day with pencils and paper and make out the schedule, and then Guy said that they had better go. Just as they were taking the rhubarb leaves off Hesperus, Daddy came along the road.

He saw us in the orchard and came in. I suddenly

remembered that Sally and the puppies were wearing his handkerchiefs, and Cavalier, who had gone off grazing, was still in his bathing wrap.

Daddy said, 'Good heavens, what's all this?' and I explained that it was a party in honour of Cavalier. He looked at the people and said, 'You seem to have borrowed a good deal from my wardrobe,' and he laughed. He seemed in a very good temper, and afterwards I knew why.

The cousins went away and I undressed the people. The puppies were in a partyish mood, and I had a job to get them back to the harness room, but the bantams seemed glad to go. Birds are all right and useful about eggs, but they can't join in your joys and sorrows as horses and dogs do.

When everyone was undressed I put the rhubarb leaves on the bonfire and took the clothes indoors. The handkerchiefs had got rather crumpled so I thought that I had better iron them. I had just put the iron on the range when Mummy called me.

I went into the drawing-room wondering if it was about the bathing wrap, but I saw at once that Mummy was looking pleased.

'Oh, Jean,' she said, 'Daddy has such splendid news.'

'What is it?' I said.

Mummy said, 'Guess.'

I guessed, 'Somebody has given us another pony,' and Mummy said, 'No.'

I guessed a horse and a foal and a dog and a cow, but each time Mummy said 'No.'

'Well, I don't know what it can be,' I said, and then I suddenly had an idea and said, 'There's going to be another gymkhana!'

Mummy said 'No' again, and Daddy said, 'Can't you think of anything else we'd all like?' but I couldn't, so he said, 'Well, I'll tell you. We're going to be well off again.'

'Well off?' I said.

'Yes, you donkey, rich,' said Mummy. 'At least not really rich but nearly as well off as we used to be. Daddy's had a marvellous job offered him.'

I couldn't say anything. I felt perfectly awful. They were pleased – actually pleased – that we were going back to being as we were before we came to the country, and had Cavalier, and the dogs, and hens and things. I thought of London and the large proper house with no orchard, and the dull old walks in Kensington Gardens, and poor darling Shadow with the London dust on his paws. I thought of leaving the cottage and the apple trees and the long grass, and of having no hens or bantams but only the Serpentine ducks that didn't belong to us at all. I knew that Mummy would buy me smart clothes that pricked and were tight, and that I should have to wear socks and a hat, and I knew that even if I was at school in term time she would get me a holiday governess, who would take me out for walks and improve my French accent and say, 'Don't swing your arms,' and 'Hold your head up,' and 'Don't kick your ankles.' The worst thing of all was that I knew I couldn't have Cavalier in London. When I thought of that I felt too awful. I felt like bursting, and finally I did. I sat down on the floor and *howled*.

Mummy said, 'Jean, *darling!*'

Daddy said, 'What on earth's the matter with the child?'

I managed to howl out that I didn't want to be rich and go back to London and walk in Kensington Gardens and have beastly clothes. I said, 'I want to stay here with the hens and the puppies.' Somehow I *couldn't* say anything about Cavalier.

Mummy said, 'My dear idiot, stop that fiendish noise and listen. We're not going back to London. We're going to keep the cottage and get some more land with it and build on. You'd like to have the stable floor repaired, wouldn't you, and you'd like a teak bucket instead of a tin one, wouldn't you, and lots of apples and carrots for Cavalier? We *may* have a tiny flat in London to go to in the winter, but I can promise you that we'll spend all your holidays here. You were going to school in September anyhow, and now you'll be able to go to Castlethorpe instead of a cheaper school.' Castlethorpe is the school where Mummy was, and until we got poor I had always been told that I was going there.

Daddy said, 'I don't suppose that now she knows her dear little cousin, she'll want to go.'

Camilla is at Castlethorpe.

I thought about Camilla and I thought about the children I had known in London. Camilla was scornful, but at any rate she liked ponies; she didn't play with dolls' prams, or ride a fairy cycle, or shriek for Nannie, or have a night light, and she hadn't got curls. I said, 'Oh, well, Camilla isn't so bad. She only wants sitting on.'

Daddy said, 'You surprise me.' He often says that to me. I don't know why.

Then Mummy and I went to dish up the dinner. When I saw the iron I remembered that I had left it on the range. It was red hot now and glowed. But Mummy said that it didn't matter. She said that the handkerchiefs could go to the laundry.

I sat up to dinner that night and we talked about the things we should buy. I said I should have a riding coat and rugs for Cavalier and the stable repaired and tiles round the manger like the cousins have in their stable, only blue instead of green. Daddy and Mummy were going to buy a car and some land and build on it. But they weren't going to spoil the cottage with a horrible garage. The cottage next to us had been empty ever since we came, so they were going to buy that and use it for a married couple, who'd be nice and let me cook when I wanted to. There is a barn next to the cottage and they thought they would repair that and make it into a garage, and the loft would do as a workshop to make hen coops in.

When we had finished dinner and decided everything, we washed up, and then I went out into the orchard to say good-night to Cavalier. I did feel happy. It was lovely to think that though we were rich again, which Daddy and Mummy like, I needn't ever go back to London, but could always stay in the country and have all the things I wanted for Cavalier. The fright that I had had in the drawing-room when they had told me that we were rich again, had made everything seem lovelier than ever, and I walked round the orchard just for the pleasure of feeling the grass flip against my bare legs – it was wet already

'CAMILLA IS AT CASTLETHORPE'

with the dew. Cavalier came behind me, and we went and looked at the moon in the duck pond. We could hear the hens making sleepy twittering noises in the hen house and Mr Higgins' lambs bleating up at the farm.

It was funny to think that if we had never been poor we should never have had all this. Proverbs are irritating, especially when grown-ups use them to make you do things – like 'a stitch in time saves nine' to make you darn your stockings, and 'procrastination is the thief of time' to make you sit down at once and write to say thank you for your birthday presents; but I did say 'it's an ill wind that blows nobody good' to Cavalier as we looked at the moon in the duck pond. If pepper hadn't gone wrong, we should never have come to the country, and the cousins would never have had us to tea and suggested that the poor Toastrack, that they had bought out of kindness, 'would do, for a bit anyhow, as a pony for Jean.'

I will finish this story with Cavalier and me looking at the moon in the duck pond because, as I have said before, it must not be too expensive. Ten shillings is what one's aunt usually sends one, and one does not want to spend it all on one thing. Perhaps one day I will write another book and tell you what happened afterwards, or perhaps they will make me work so hard and do so many exams at Castlethorpe that I shall never want to write a word again.

Joanna Cannan

Joanna Cannan (1896–1961) wrote thirty-eight books – for children, detective fiction and novels. Brought up in Oxford where her father was a university dean, she was proud of her Scottish ancestry and spent holidays in the Highlands. Here she came to love a life more adventurous than usual for girls of the time, rambling and mountain climbing. During the first world war she was a nurse and met and married Harold Pullein-Thompson, a captain in the army. He was wounded in the war and she shared in supporting their family, of Denis – who became a playwright – and their daughters Josephine, Christine and Diana.

It was their life in the Oxfordshire countryside, in a rambling house with cats, dogs, bantams and ponies that provided the background to the three sisters' well-loved pony books. But it was Joanna who created this kind of book with A PONY FOR JEAN, introducing a determined and resourceful girl with an unpromising pony.

Anne Bullen

Anne Bullen (1913–1963) was born in Hampshire, but grew up in Somerset amongst horses and ponies. In 1933 Anne married, and she moved to Dorset where she brought up six children with her husband, Jack. Her romantic and versatile illustrative style caught the eye of Joanna Cannan, who gave Anne her first commission to illustrate A PONY FOR JEAN. Other authors followed suit, and Anne illustrated over forty books as well as three of her own. Anne and her husband also ran a very successful stud farm (The Catherston Stud), and although Anne very sadly died aged 51, she was able to watch her son compete at the Rome Olympics, the first of three Bullens to ride in seven consecutive Olympic Games.